Katie's Keepsake
Book Seven in Clover Creek Caravan
Kirsten Osbourne

Sign up for instant notification of all of Kirsten's New Releases Text 'BOB' to 42828

And

For a complete list of Kirsten's works head to her website wwww.kirstenandmorganna.com

Chapter One

Friday, June 26th, 1852

We are moving again today after staying over for a full day due to the rainstorm and mud. I hope we won't have many more unplanned stops. I feel like we're losing the advantage we have by leaving before anyone else did. Today is George's first day driving again after almost drowning to save my Anna. I still feel like I owe him so much. Losing my husband was bad enough but losing my little girl would have cut my heart right out of my chest.

All three Bedwell men will be sharing our meals with us, and I hope my children get to the point where they don't run away from George when he talks to them. The man is harsh, but he treats my children the same as he treats his own. I've found his boys like to hide when he speaks to them as well.

George simply doesn't seem to know how to talk to people. He's gruff to the point of rudeness, but I have no problem standing up to him. Perhaps that's why he seems to respect me more than others. I have no idea. I do know that I yearn for a way to repay his kindness. There must be a way.

Now that the day's walk was over, Katie waited as Stanley unhitched the team of oxen and put them into pasture with the others. There was always a small area where the oxen were kept when they stopped, and this stop was no different. Men took turns guarding the livestock, and others would guard the people. There was no true danger from the Indians, from what Katie had heard, but there was worry they would steal the animals.

Katie squatted beside the fire she'd started with the buffalo chips the children had brought to her. There was an ingenious way to find the chips. Each child carried a long stick, and they would poke the stick into a buffalo mess. If the stick came out clean, it was safe to collect. If it didn't, no one wanted it in camp. She was always pleased to think that the manure left by their cows, horses, and oxen would later be fuel for another family along the trail.

As she started supper for her own four children as well as George and his two boys, her mind was still on her husband. He'd been buried right on the trail so other wagons would drive over it and his scent wouldn't be there when wolves came sniffing around. But to just leave him...if it hadn't been for her children, she would have crawled right into the grave with her dear Ned.

Supper was a simple pot of beans with chunks of bacon cut up in them. And she'd make a sweet cornbread to go with it. The children wouldn't be thrilled with the meal, but their bellies would be full, and they'd be nourished. That's all Katie worried about.

Anna came to her putting a small pile of buffalo chips beside her. "Is that enough, Mama? May I play with my friends now?"

Katie smiled at the little girl she'd almost lost. It was hard now to look at her and not see her in the water, struggling to keep her head above it. She was so grateful to still have the child. This journey had been full of so much death and despair, but she couldn't turn back. She had to get the land Ned had wanted so she and her children could live a good life.

"Of course, you may play with your friends now. Have Mrs. Prewitt send you back at suppertime."

"Yes, Mama!" And little Anna was off to play with Amanda and Sally, and all the other children who had started to gather around their wagon when they were in camp.

George joined her looking a bit gray. Perhaps the doctor had been wrong, and he'd gone back to driving too soon. "Are you feeling all right?"

George took a seat on a rock beside the fire. "I'm very tired, and I'll probably turn in shortly after supper." He shook his head. "Something I could do just weeks ago is much too difficult now. I feel like half a man."

"Do you think you're driving too soon?" she asked. "I can get the doctor!"

He grunted. "I don't need a doctor. I just need to sit a spell. Stop treating me like one of your children, Katie."

Katie smiled at that. "I can't. I've spent so much time taking care of you that I can't help but worry about you."

"Well, I don't need to be taken care of now." He looked annoyed with her, but Katie didn't mind. He was always annoyed with someone. He looked at the pot. "Beans for supper? Have I told you how sick I am of beans?"

She shrugged. "They keep better than anything else. If you want to eat, then we'll eat the beans we brought with us, and be thankful that God has provided." Smiling a little, Katie tilted her head to one side. "Imagine how the Israelites felt when they were lost in the wilderness, with nothing but manna to eat. I make beans less than half the time, and I feel very thankful."

George sighed. "I should have known you'd use my complaints as a lesson in how to be a Christian. You are a good woman, Katie."

"I try to be." Katie stood up and stretched. There was only one more day of walking before their day of rest, and despite having a day of rest yesterday, she just needed another soon. She couldn't voice it though, because George liked to latch onto anything negative and make it a million times worse. "Where are your boys?"

He shrugged. "They took their rifles and went off in search of game. They're tired of eating so many beans as well, despite the fact that we get a change from our version of manna on occasion."

She smiled. "I'll tell you what. You boys get me some meat, and I'll make us a nice stew, or a roast if there's a lot of it. I would love to be able to cook more creatively, but at the moment, I have to ration our meat, so we're going to eat the beans we have, and thank God for every bite."

George sighed. "So, what you're saying is I need to do my part and get out there and shoot a buffalo."

Katie shook her head. "Not at all. What I'm saying is if we get meat, we'll be thankful, but if we keep eating our beans, we'll be thankful for those as well."

His boys and her son Stanley walked back into camp then. "Three rabbits," George's fifteen-year-old son, Harvey said. "Can we have them for supper tomorrow instead of beans?"

She nodded enthusiastically. "Get them skinned and cleaned, and I'll happily turn them into the best stew you ever tasted!" Katie was used to cooking creatively. Ned had worked for a factory back in Pennsylvania, and there had never been enough money to buy what they wanted, so she had learned to cook just about anything, including the squirrels Stanley would bring her for their meals.

The boys grinned. "We'll have them back in a few minutes, Ma!" Stanley led the other boys away, obviously thinking they'd find a stream or something.

"There's no water along here!" George called after them. "You boys need to use the sense God gave a goose."

Katie frowned at George before smiling at the boys. "Use as little of our water stores as you can. We can't refill for a day or two."

Stanley nodded. "Yes, Ma."

Harvey looked between his father and Katie. "We'll use our water stores, since yours are used for cooking and dishes, Mrs. Gilbert."

She smiled. "Good thinking, Harvey. Thank you!" As the boys hurried away, she looked at her daughter's savior and wanted to throttle him. "You don't have to yell at the boys constantly, you know. You could easily have told them to use water stores without insulting them."

George sighed. "Patience never complained about how I talked to my boys."

"Patience was afraid of you. Everyone in camp says she was. I'm not. You're not to be rude to my children again. I don't think you should be rude to yours either, but I can't control how you treat your own sons." She stood up, wishing she knew how to get through to him. Walking to the back of the wagon, she pulled out what she needed to make the cornbread for supper. She'd have to make a double batch because of their company, but George was sharing his food storage with her as well.

"My boys don't mind how I talk to them!"

Katie shook her head. "When you were sick, they'd hide from you, rather than coming around. I was the only one who could stand being around you."

"That can't be true. My boys respect me."

"Your boys fear you. That fear is the only reason they obey. There's not one lick of respect for you at all." Putting the mixed cornbread onto the fire, she smiled. "There. Everything will be ready soon, and we can all eat."

"Katie, why do you tell me all about my failings instead of being afraid of me like everyone else in this camp? Sometimes I wish you'd keep your thoughts to yourself." George was used to fear, and he preferred it because people were less likely to insult him.

Katie shrugged. "Someone needs to tell you like it is. If no one else will, I'll be here, ready to tell you all sorts of things you'd rather not listen to."

George got to his feet. "Sometimes you make me crazy."

"Sometimes I want to throw rocks at your head," Katie responded. She would never back down from the man. She'd seen how he treated women who did, and she wasn't about to be one of them.

"That's not very kind!"

"I try to be a good Christian woman, but there are times, I think you were put on this earth to test me." She wiped her hands dry, and moved to the back of the wagon again, pulling out the dishes they'd eat with.

The boys all stayed away until Katie raised her arm to get their attention and bring them back to her fire. Anna was the first to come back. She was afraid of the former captain, but she knew he'd saved her life, so she had a lot more patience with him than the rest of them did.

"Did you make your delicious cornbread to go with the yucky beans, Mama?"

Katie smiled at her daughter. "Of course, I did. I wouldn't ask you to eat yucky beans unless you could sop them up with delicious cornbread."

At Anna's toothless grin, Katie laughed. She couldn't help herself. Her daughter simply looked funny without her four front teeth. All her boys had lost their bottom teeth and then months later their top teeth. Not Anna. She'd lost all four in the same week. "You fill me with joy, Anna Joy!"

"It's my job," Anna said. "You gave me Joy for my name!"

The five boys trickled into camp then. Stanley, Phillip, who was nine, and Gregory who was eleven, all belonged to Katie. Harvey, who was fifteen, and Albert who was twelve, belonged to George and his late wife.

"Stanley, would you say the prayer over our meal?" Katie asked her son. She knew George and his boys didn't often make it to the church service in camp, and she could only imagine the type of prayer George would come up with.

"Sure, Ma." Stanley bowed his head and prayed for all of them. "Thank you for this meal. We appreciate that we have beans to eat when there's little fresh meat. You always provide. In your son Jesus's name. Amen."

Katie smiled at her eldest son. "That was a fine prayer." And then she was busy dishing out beans and cornbread to all the children and George, and lastly to herself.

While they ate, her children complimented her on the meal, all of them mentioning the cornbread in particular. The first time she'd cooked for George's boys, they'd complained, but they'd learned from her own children. "This is really good, Mrs. Gabriel," Harvey said.

"Thank you, Harvey."

Albert nodded. "So much better than when Pa tried to make beans for us. They got burned, and we had to eat them or go hungry." George glared at his son, who immediately ducked his head. "Sorry, Pa."

"You know better than to insult me in public!"

Albert nodded, refusing to look up. "I'm very sorry."

Katie watched it and shook her head. "When we first started on the trail, I needed to learn to cook some things all over again. I was used to cooking on our stove in Pennsylvania, and it was difficult to learn to cook over an open fire."

Stanley nodded. "I remember you made some of your cornbread that even the dog wouldn't try."

"You brought a dog?" George asked, obviously distracted by her admission she'd had to learn to cook all over again.

Katie nodded. "She was old, and we knew she wouldn't make it, but we brought her with us anyway. We thought she deserved to be with the people she loved in her last days. She died before we even reached Independence."

She missed the dog with everything inside her. She'd gotten Pepper as a puppy when she was first married.

Anna sighed, patting her mother's arm. "I miss her too, Mama."

"She was a good dog," Gregory agreed.

As she finished eating, Katie walked to the fire where she'd already started water heating to wash the dishes. It was much less water than she would have liked to use, but it would be at least another day before they reached water, and she wasn't going to waste what they did have. Instead, she'd be thankful they had some and use the water as sparingly as she could.

Anna walked around and gathered the dishes the boys had used and took them to her mother, but she left George with his bowl, which wasn't empty yet. Katie knew he was trying to get out of eating the beans, but she also knew he needed the nourishment that came from eating it all. "I'd like to see you finish it, George," she said softly.

He grunted but ate another bite of the beans. "I'm looking forward to that rabbit for tomorrow."

Katie smiled. "I am as well. I think I'll cut it up and make a nice thick stew out of it."

Stanley sighed. "I cannot wait. Ma makes the best rabbit stew in all of the west."

"You boys go. Maybe you can kill a couple of more rabbits before bed. Come back as soon as it starts getting dark."

All five of the boys stood and hurried away, grabbing rifles, and in Phillip's case a sling shot. Katie knew from experience he would find rocks along the way.

As soon as the dishes were finished and stashed in the back of the wagon, Anna looked at her mother, who nodded at her. Anna knew that meant she would be able to run and enjoy her evening until bedtime. She'd done her chores for the day.

George looked around him at how quickly the camp had emptied. "How do you get my boys to obey you so well?" he asked. He'd always fought with his boys and had to resort to threats.

"They respect me. And they know I'm cooking for them. None of them are going to risk not having food to eat. I do hope they can get two or three more rabbits, though. I think we could all eat our fill if they manage more." Katie smiled, thinking about how nice it would be to have a full belly for a change. She often didn't eat as much as she gave her children.

"Would you like to walk with me?" George asked her. He'd seen so many courting couples walk together in the evenings. Perhaps she would allow him to court her. It was what he wanted. Katie was special, and she could talk back to him without being afraid. For so long, Patience had kept her head down, afraid to even meet his eyes. It had gotten to the point where he had little respect for her.

Katie nodded. "I think that would be good for you. You need to keep your exercises up so you can regain your strength."

George walked away from the center of camp, not reaching out to touch her, because that would be improper. He did carry his rifle over one shoulder, praying he could get one of the rabbits, or perhaps even a deer.

"Everyone in camp blames me for my wife's death," he said softly, surprising her.

Katie had heard the stories, but never from him. "What happened?"

"Patience wasn't a strong woman," George said softly. "She begged me for years not to force her to go west with me. I made the journey once without her, and then I decided we were all going, whether she liked it or not."

"I know most women go west only because their husbands force them." It hadn't been the case with her and Ned. She'd readily agreed to go, knowing it would help him to live out his lifelong dream of having a ranch. He'd never liked the factory work he was forced to do to feed his family.

"Patience was ill a lot. She kept losing babies, and I thought it was simply because she was babied back home. She had a maid who did for the family, so she didn't need to." He shook his head. "So, I made her leave behind everything and everyone she'd ever known. She cried something fierce, but I wouldn't even let her bring the maid along."

"Was she really too weak?" Katie asked, feeling badly for the other woman.

"She was, but I didn't believe it. We hadn't been on the road long when I told her she wasn't going to spend any more afternoons sleeping in the wagon. I thought it would be good for her to get to know some of the other women." He frowned. "Instead, she stepped on a rattler, and she was killed almost instantly."

Katie put her hand on his arm in commiseration. "I'm so sorry for your loss."

He looked at her again, thinking for the third time in as many hours about what a good woman she was. He didn't deserve to have her as a friend.

Chapter Two

Saturday, June 27th, 1852

We were able to move faster than expected today, and at the end of our journey for the week, we found ourselves passing through three crossings. It's where we cross three rivers in the matter of a few miles. The captains made a smart decision to camp right after the third crossing. At one point the wall of granite beside us pressed so close there was only room for one wagon at a time.

Soon after we stopped, many of the members of the wagon train ventured over to carve their names in the granite wall, just as they did at Independence Rock. How many places do emigrants' names need to be carved on a two-thousand mile journey? It seems to me they waste their time and effort forever carving their names. What they should be doing is hunting and making sure there's food for their families. I do not understand wasting time the way many of our company do.

I myself would have taken the company through the south pass. Yes, it's mainly sand, but it's a bit faster and would have been the best choice for us. I suppose the new captains are frightened enough of going without water, they do whatever they can to appease their sniveling women.

George climbed down from his wagon, and Harvey rushed over to take care of the oxen. George was thankful his wife had insisted they wait a year before heading west, because his boys were big enough and strong enough to be of some real help. As he watched Harvey walk away from him, he realized his son was becoming a man right before his eyes. It was hard for George to think about.

Walking straight to Katie's wagon seemed to be the right thing to do. He knew she was unsure of him in many ways, but he also knew he was determined to marry her and make her his.

He walked to the fire she'd already started. He was always amazed at how very efficient the woman was with everything she did. She was a marvel in so many ways. He'd rarely admired a woman before, but this one...well, she was different. She took her tasks as seriously as any man he'd ever known, and she was so brave in the face of spending the rest of her life with no man at her side and being left with four children to care for.

Katie smiled at him, and it was as if a second sun had come up in the sky to truly light the world. "I'm making the rabbit stew. With the seven rabbits the boys got yesterday, I should be able to make it very hearty."

"Stew sounds wonderful. Of course, you can even make the dreaded beans taste decent."

Katie seemed surprised at the compliment. "Why, thank you, George."

The children came then, bringing their daily allotment of buffalo chips so they could use them for the fire. "May we play now?" Phillip asked.

At Katie's nod, he grabbed his slingshot, and all the children scattered. Katie sometimes missed talking to her own children when George was around, because they certainly wouldn't stay with her if he was there.

"You should make them do more," George admonished. "Your girl is big enough to be helping you with the cooking."

Katie smiled. "Anna helps with the dishes every evening, and she gathers buffalo chips to burn. I won't ask more from her when she has such good friends she can play with in the evenings." She couldn't help but wonder why George wouldn't take a moment to learn her children's names, but he never had. His disdain for most women and children was obvious. At times she wanted to tell him that he couldn't eat with her family because of how he acted, but so far, a word from her had him acting civil.

"You spoil them all, Katie. Mark my words, they're going to have a hard time doing the work you need them to do once we actually reach our new homesteads."

Katie shrugged. "I'll retrain them then. The trail is hard on everyone, even the children."

He watched her as she peeled and cut up carrots, potatoes, and chopped up the rabbits for her stew. "That's going to be a big pot of food."

She smiled, and again, he felt as if the entire world was brighter. "We'll have enough for all of us to eat our fill tonight, and again at noontime tomorrow. I feel so thankful the boys were blessed with these rabbits, and in turn, we will be blessed with full bellies for a change."

He shrugged. "I sure had my fill of the beans last night."

Katie laughed at that. "We've all had a lifetime worth of beans, but tonight, we'll be able to eat a meal we actually enjoy and get our fill. That will be amazing for us."

George shook his head. "Is there anything you won't find a bright side to?"

She pursed her lips. "To be honest, when I was sure Ned would die, I couldn't see any brightness at all. There I was alone in the middle of the prairie with my children and no one else around. I couldn't even legally live there, but I was going to try. I had to have a roof over my children's heads and food in their bellies. I would have done anything to make it happen, but I felt like I was plodding alone in the dark."

He frowned. "I'm so sorry it's hard on you. Losing Patience made me feel guilty for not listening to her that she needed to ride that afternoon, and I miss her, but I never felt like I was lost without her."

"Then you didn't truly love her," Katie said, stopping peeling a potato for a moment and staring into the fire. She felt badly for Patience that she'd never been loved, but even worse for George, because with the way he talked, she doubted he would ever find the kind of love she'd shared with Ned. She couldn't imagine a woman putting up with him and the way he treated others.

As soon as everyone was gathered for supper, Katie's Phillip said the prayer for their meal, and they all ate their fill. "We haven't been able to eat this much ever!" Anna said excitedly.

Katie laughed. They had always had plenty as long as she'd been able to get a good kitchen garden going. There were of course times when food was scarcer, but she doubted Anna really remembered them. "The boys did a good job getting enough rabbits for us to have a hearty meal for a change."

"I'll gladly help with the dishes if you keep making food like this, Mama."

"You always help with the dishes with a smile on your face, Anna. You're a good helper."

Anna seemed to grow five inches with the compliment. George stared at the child. He wondered if something like that would work for him. "You're really good at collecting buffalo chips for the fires as well."

The entire group went silent, and everyone was glancing at one another as if to see what was wrong. Finally, Anna gave him a leery smile. "Thank you, Mr. Bedwell."

George couldn't help but wonder why they'd reacted so differently to the compliments from him than they had from Katie. They took Katie's words for granted, but his? It seemed as if he frightened them all.

After supper, Anna helped with the dishes, as usual. When she ran off to play, George asked about the reaction. "Why did everyone seem almost frightened when I complimented Anna? They seem to expect it from you, but never from me."

"That's the thing, George. The children *do* expect compliments from me. They receive them often. Your words are more scathing. You teach the boys, but you do it through fear and not through love."

He bristled. "Are you saying I don't love my boys?"

"Of course not. I would never say that. You simply don't *show* them love."

"A man doesn't need to show his love to his boys. He teaches through strength."

"Ned was always telling the boys he loved them and was proud of them. When Stanley started driving after Ned's accident, Ned made sure to tell him constantly how proud he was, and that he'd be a good provider if Ned died. Stanley didn't want to see his pa die anymore than I did, but he seemed to understand that he was capable, thanks to Ned's words."

"Treating a boy like that makes him a Nancy boy."

Katie sighed. "No, it doesn't. It makes him strong because he knows he's loved."

"My boys know I love them."

She shook her head. "No, they know you will take care of them. They're two very different things."

"And your way of parenting is better than mine, I guess?" George felt the anger rising up inside him, but he knew he couldn't let it show. Katie was the only woman he'd ever met who would stand up to him, and if he tried to show her his anger, she would simply refuse to listen. He couldn't help but admire her, even as he felt anger toward her.

"I honestly don't know which is better, but I know what I want for my children. I want them to feel as if I'll love them no matter what happens to them. I want them to know I'm here for them."

"My boys know that."

"Do they?"

George glared at her for a moment. "The dancing is about to start. Let's go join the others."

Katie looked at him with surprise. "You never join the others for dancing."

"I will tonight unless that bothers you as well." George didn't like her criticism of him, but he realized that his boys probably didn't like to be criticized either. Maybe it was time to learn more from her.

As they walked to the area where the dancing would take place, Katie watched George as he avoided talking to anyone else. The other women came to her and talked and laughed with her. Betty was the only bold one who looked at the former captain and smiled. "You seem to be feeling much better, Mr. Bedwell."

George simply nodded. "Thanks to the expert care of Mrs. Gabriel, I believe I am."

Katie realized then that she was the only person she'd ever heard George compliment until supper that evening. Maybe the man was softening. He needed to if he didn't want to spend the rest of his life alone.

Once they were sitting on the ground—no previous groups had built benches there—he turned to her. "I don't think I'll be able to dance this evening, but I thought perhaps we could enjoy watching the others."

"I appreciate that. I do enjoy watching the children dance. That Edna girl in particular."

George made a face. "I don't believe I would have allowed her family to come if I'd realized how simple she was."

Katie shook her head. "I don't think she's simple. I think she enjoys life to the fullest, and she's not afraid to say what she thinks. I find her very endearing."

"I'm not so sure," George said, shaking his head.

She couldn't help but smile at that. "I am."

The music was lively, and she enjoyed watching the children dance. One of the Cauldron twins took Anna's hand and led her to the makeshift dancefloor. Though Katie was wary of the boys, she thought it was sweet when he bowed low to Anna, and she curtsied.

Katie watched them closely, but the children seemed to simply enjoy the dance. She spotted little Amanda Bolling with the boy's twin. She hadn't yet learned to tell them apart, but they weren't completely identical. She'd have to ask Mrs. Cauldron for advice on telling the differences between them later.

She leaned toward George and said softly, "I will let Anna choose her own husband, as long as it's not one of the Cauldron twins. Those boys are hellions."

George chuckled. "You never know. One of them might grow up to be a preacher."

Katie shook her head. She believed a child could be anything, but a Cauldron boy becoming a preacher? That would be like asking the earth to open up and rivers to flow in every direction. It was impossible to even consider. "Not those boys."

After the dancing had stopped, Katie gathered her children. "Let's get back to our fire and get ready for bed. Tomorrow is our day of rest, which means I will spend it working in camp." She didn't mind having to do the laundry on Sundays as long as they didn't have to walk. She didn't know why one felt like it was all right and the other didn't, but it's how she'd felt since they'd first left.

Of course, her last company had planned to move every day to beat the snows. She knew it was important to not get caught in the storms, but it was more important to worship her God.

Back in camp, Anna sat down with Katie. "Is Mr. Bedwell going to be our new pa?"

Katie's eyes grew wide. "No, sweetie. Of course not! I'm only watching out for him because he saved you from the river."

Anna nodded, but Stanley walked up behind them. "I'm not sure, Ma. I've seen him watching you when you're not looking. I think perhaps he's thinking of you in a way you don't think of him."

Katie shook her head. "I don't think so. He's not a man to look at any woman as if she's special."

"I think he is. I heard all the stories about him killing his wife and all that, but Harvey and Albert say that he loves you like he never loved their ma."

"And how would it make you feel if I did marry him then?" There was no way she would ever do it, but it was interesting to hear her children's view on the subject.

Stanley shrugged. "He's really different than pa, but he seems to be getting better. He doesn't yell at us anymore, and he's yelling at his own sons less. Maybe you're teaching him how to love people and not yell like he used to."

"I'm not so sure about that..." Katie was surprised to hear what Stanley was saying, but when she thought about it, he did seem to have softened around his children and hers. Did that mean he was actually changing? Or was he simply trying to be nice because she'd nursed him for so long?

Maybe there was hope for George Bedwell yet, but not with her. No, he couldn't marry a woman with children. He still had trouble figuring out how he should treat them.

As the children went to bed, she thought about her duties for the next day. She needed to make supper—and hopefully someone would get some meat, so it could be a fresh meat supper—make breakfast, and she could serve the leftovers from supper for the noon meal. Then she had to do the wash for the week down at the stream with the other woman, and make sure everything in the wagon was tidy. She needed to go through George's supplies as well to see if she could supplement her flour and sugar with what he had left.

Worrying about the food she had left wouldn't help. They'd purchased enough for a family of six, and without Ned, they should have more than enough to make it to Oregon.

If they were able to get some buffalo, then she and the other ladies would spend the day together, smoking and drying the meat. But oh, a couple of fresh meals would feel heavenly. Perhaps it was possible, but she could never count on the luck that it took to bring the meat in.

No, she'd plan to make beans after they had two hearty meals of rabbit stew, and they could complain all they wanted. Beans were filling, and if the children didn't go hungry, that was the most important thing to her.

Then, as she did at the end of every day, she had a little talk with Ned. Some said that your loved ones watched over you after they passed on, and she wasn't sure she believed it, but it did make her feel better to talk to her dead husband.

I miss you so much, Ned. The children are asking if I'll marry again, and even suggesting the man I told you about, George Bedwell. Remember, he's the one who saved our Anna from drowning in the river. I thought he was a horrible man, but the children have pointed out that spending time with me has made him softer. It's strange to think about, and I'm still not sure I believe it, but they don't sound like they'd be opposed.

Don't worry, though. You are my one true love, and if I did something like that, it would only be to help the children. I worry that once we reach Oregon, I won't be able to provide for them. I suppose I could offer to cook meals to travelers, but I want to follow your dream and start the ranch you always wanted. I don't see why I can't. Stanley really thinks he could run the ranch, and the other boys are willing to help.

Anna says she'll do all the chores. We both know our Anna doesn't know how to do all the chores, and she wouldn't if she did. The girl is still flighty, but I do love having a girl finally. She helps with the dishes every night without complaining, and she has even gotten good at finding the buffalo chips for my fire.

All the children have surprised me, growing up so much since you passed on. It sure does help, but I wish my babies wouldn't grow up so fast. They're all I have left of you, Ned.

I wish I could just have one more kiss. One more embrace. I never dreamed what life would be like without you, and I know it couldn't have been as bleak as reality has been. But as you asked, I keep smiling for the children.

It does grow a little easier every day, but nighttime is hard for me. I want to feel your loving arms around me and feel you press a kiss onto my cheek as I fall asleep with you holding me. Life will never be the same without you, but you had a dream, and I will do all I can to make that dream come true.

Goodnight, Ned. I will never stop loving you.

Chapter Three

Sunday, June 28th, 1852

I'm so thankful that today is our day of rest. When Ned first wanted to go on the trail, I was worried about all the extra work I would face, but then I gradually became excited to start a new life with him, ranching like he has always wanted. After he died, I went back to thinking about all the extra work involved with the trail. The children help as much as they can, both with hunting and helping around the camp. I do wish Anna was a little older and could help more, but I also don't want to wish away her wonder at everything around us. She is my last child and thinking about her growing up leaves my heart sad.

We had a delicious supper of rabbit stew last night that was more than enough for our family as well as the Bedwells. I do hope that we can get more fresh meat today. The men have all gone to hunt this afternoon, while we women stay in camp and see to chores that must be done, such as laundry. The boys are willing to jump in the creek here with their clothing on, and they say they will get just as clean, but I don't believe them one bit. Instead, I'll wash their clothes for them.

The habits my boys have picked up on this trail are truly appalling, and I know it will be all I can do to retrain them to be gentleman once we reach Oregon City. My family has been asked by the others in camp to settle with them, and we can continue to help one another the way we have done on the trail. As long as the rest of us arrive in one piece, I will settle anywhere. Thankfully, we are over halfway now, and the children are all well. I pray every day the Lord will keep them safe for the rest of our journey.

Now, I must do the laundry, and I will say an extra prayer that the men get fresh meat. I can make do with the jerky we have, but it is so nice when we actually have something fresh to eat.

Katie carried the dirty clothes she and her children had worn that week down to the creek, thankful there was a place to wash. They hadn't expected to go quite as far as they had the previous day, and they were all delighted to be able to refill their water barrels and have a place to wash their clothes.

She knelt at the side of the creek beside Mrs. Davies, who seemed to be handling the loss of her husband as well as anyone. Katie understood the look on the other woman's face, and she just wanted to gather her into her arms and hold her, telling her everything would be all right. But they both knew that wasn't true.

"What can I do to help you?" Katie asked, looking at the other woman.

Mrs. Davies's eyes filled with tears. "There's nothing anyone can do. I still can't believe my poor Adam was trampled by the very buffalo he was trying to kill for our supper." She dashed the tears away with the back of her arm, her hands covered with soap and water from her own laundry.

"I understand. My Ned was lost in just a couple of days. We were certain we would be alone on the prairie for the rest of our days."

"I'm glad the captains didn't feel the need to leave me behind. I don't know what I would do." Mrs. Davies rested her hand on her abdomen. "I was waiting for our next meal with fresh meat to tell him I was expecting. He died without knowing."

Katie's heart went out to the girl beside her. "I'm sure he knows. If you find you need help with anything, you let me know. The trail is hard on all women, but if you are in the family way, I can only imagine it will be so much worse. I'm willing to do whatever it takes to make your days easier."

"Thank you," Mrs. Davies said, trying to smile, but it looked like a mockery of happiness more than anything else.

"How are you handling driving your wagon while pregnant? The last couple of days must have been particularly hard on you."

Mrs. Davies nodded. "I never liked driving even when I wasn't expecting. But now? It feels like my arms are going to fall off, and I'm so tired." She shook her head. "Never in my life have I wanted to nap as badly as I have the past couple of weeks."

Katie frowned. "I may have a way I can help. Let me talk to some people, and I'll let you know later. And I'd love for you to join us at our campfire for supper tonight. You shouldn't have to cook after doing laundry all day."

Mrs. Davies smiled slightly. "That would actually be really nice if you don't mind."

"I'll warn you now, the former captain eats with my family every evening. I hope you won't mind."

"I think I can handle that. All three of us have lost loved ones on the trail, after all."

Katie wasn't certain that George had lost someone he loved. It sounded to her as if Patience was just a woman he took for granted, though she hoped that wasn't true. Everyone deserved love. "I usually stand with my hand up to call everyone to supper. I'm certain you'll see it."

"Thank you again for inviting me. I didn't even make it to our church service today because I didn't want to see or talk to anyone. I appreciate your kindness." Mrs. Davies rinsed out her husband's extra pair of pants. "I don't even know what I'm going to do with these, but I'm keeping them. Someone will need britches, and I can provide a pair."

Katie smiled at that. "I still have my husband's spare clothes as well. I can't imagine getting rid of them. Though I've heard we can trade with the Indians at Fort Bridger." She finished scrubbing Anna's spare dress. She'd brought two changes of clothes for everyone. "I'm Katie, by the way."

"I'm Jane."

"May I use your Christian name?" Katie asked. She knew not many of the women had gotten close to the new widow.

"Absolutely. And I'll use yours."

Katie smiled at the other woman. "I'll be watching out for you as I can."

Jane sniffled a little. "I need it. I wish I could turn right around and go back to Wisconsin and my mother, but I feel we've gone a little far for that."

"I wanted to do the same thing when Ned died. The memories don't fade, but it is a little easier to smile as I think about him every day. We're here to help with anything you need."

"Thank you." Jane finished the last of her laundry, and Katie watched her head back to her wagon. Wanting to treat her new friend as Margaret had treated her when her Ned had just died, she would be watching out as much as she could for ways to help. Even if she couldn't do something, she could easily ask someone else to help Jane.

After finishing up her laundry, Katie walked back to her wagon. It wasn't late enough to start supper, and she had her work for the day finished. She longed for a nap, but she would feel guilty for taking it. Hopefully, the men would be back soon with meat, and she would be needed to help with the drying of the meat.

Sitting down outside her wagon, she picked up her Bible and read some of Proverbs, her favorite book. It always made her feel like her mother was whispering in her ear as she read the words of advice—probably because her mother had constantly quoted from

Proverbs. Her mother hadn't been able to read, but she'd attended church every Sunday, and she'd memorized all the scriptures she could.

As soon as the thought crossed her mind, she decided she would spend the few minutes of free time to write to her parents. Her sister lived close enough that she would read the letter to them. She knew her mother would want to hear the news of Ned passing, and they would be able to mail the letter from Fort Bridger when they arrived.

Just as she took out her ink and quill, she saw some of the men come back into camp, dragging a buffalo. She had no idea who had shot the huge beast, but she knew she would be involved in drying the meat. None of the women could do it alone, not even Mary, who seemed to be able to do everything better than anyone else could.

To her surprise, the buffalo was dragged to her fire. "Mr. Bedwell shot this one. He's resting on a rock on his way back, but he'll be here soon enough. He made sure we knew to bring it to you," Mr. Prewitt, Margaret's husband, told her.

Katie covered her mouth with her hand. She would definitely share the meat, because others shared with her, but her family would get first pick of the fresh meat. Other women were gathering beside her wagon to help her get the drying done. It wasn't an easy task, and it would take them a good long while."

Margaret stood beside her. "This is your first, isn't it?"

Katie nodded, feeling so much like crying it was ridiculous. This felt like God had reached down and given her a gift that she so desperately needed to have the confidence to keep going. "We'd better get started." She said a silent prayer of thanks for the meat, and then she and the other women began the task before them. Everyone who helped would walk away with a portion of the meat in payment.

Katie noticed that Jane wasn't there helping, and when she looked around, she saw the other woman asleep under her wagon. She told herself she'd put aside a bit of the meat for her as well. Losing her husband in the first months of pregnancy had to be harder than what Katie had gone through. It would bring a lesser woman to her knees.

Because it was Katie's buffalo, the other women looked to her for direction. She took a huge roast from the beast, planning to cook it for supper, and use what was left for stew the following night. Three nights in a row with filling meals would help her family's morale a great deal.

The women worked until the buffalo had been portioned out and strips of it cut up to dry before moving on to Betty's campsite to work on the buffalo one of the young couples on the trail had shot to pay the doctor for helping the wife with childbirth.

Katie went along and helped with the slicing of the meat, listening to the doctor argue with Mr. Smith. "I know you think you owe me, but I don't take a turn with guard duty, so me helping everyone I can is my paying people back for guarding me."

Mr. Smith shook his head. "No, because you've helped my wife and I both when we were sick. Thank you for helping us, and now I no longer feel I owe you a debt. We got a good buffalo last week, and I'd be pleased with a couple of steaks for my wife to cook, but the rest is yours to do with as you will."

The doctor sighed. "All right. You'll get your steaks, and we'll call ourselves even."

Betty hadn't waited for the argument to be over, and all the women were already working on the massive buffalo. "Thank you, Doctor. I mean that. I'd do anything to make your life easier."

By the time the second buffalo was distributed and sliced to dry, it was time for Katie to start supper. Her arms ached from the work involved with drying the meat, but she would never complain. Her mother had told her that a complaining woman wasn't thankful for the blessings in her life. She was determined to always be thankful.

As soon as they were finished with the drying, Katie went back to her campfire, and put her huge roast into her Dutch oven, adding in water, carrots, and potatoes. She wished she could make biscuits with it, because it would be tasty, but she knew enough to save the flour she had for nights when she needed to stretch their meals.

When Anna hurried over to Katie to see what she was cooking, the girl squealed. "No beans!" Anna held her skirt out to both sides and spun in a circle, singing "No beans! No beans! No beans!" over and over.

Katie simply laughed and shook her head at the girl's antics. Her heart went out to Jane then because she had no children to help her learn to smile again. Katie had kept going for her children, and her forced smiles had turned into real ones. It wasn't that she didn't miss Ned every day of her life, but that she was forced to go on for her children. She hoped that Jane would be able to keep going for the baby she carried inside her.

The captain got back to camp hours after the buffalo had arrived. Katie took one look at him and poured him a cold cup of coffee. "How are you feeling?" she asked.

He shook his head. "I made myself keep up with the other men until I got my buffalo, but then I was too tired to do more."

Katie patted his hand. "I'm sorry it was so difficult for you, but I thank you for the meat. I'll use it wisely."

"Did you share with others?" he asked. He wasn't sure if he wanted her to have shared or not. It seemed that they should keep all they could for themselves, but he knew others had shared with her. Perhaps it was smart to make friends along the trail as she had.

"Of course, I did. And I saved a bit extra for Jane Davies. She's the one whose husband was trampled a few days back, and she told me today she's expecting. She'll join us for supper tonight."

The former captain nodded. "I can't imagine her having to drive those oxen when she's in the family way."

"About that...I was hoping you could spare Harvey to drive her team. I can see how hard this all is on her." Katie knew he wasn't prone to looking for ways to help others, but perhaps he would be willing to help if someone pointed out the situation to him.

"I think that's a fine idea," he said, surprising himself. "Harvey is old enough to help in a lot of different ways. Will you invite her to supper every night?"

She smiled. "I'd really like to if it's all right with you and the children. I don't know what would have happened to me if not for the kindness of others." Especially George who had seen to it that she didn't lose a child along the way.

"I think it's a fine idea. I hope you kept a large roast from that buffalo before you gave it all away."

Katie grinned. "I did. I kept a *huge* roast that will be enough for a roast and potatoes tonight and a stew tomorrow. Just think, we'll have three nights in a row with food that we like before we have to make do with beans again."

George smiled and nodded. "I'd be thrilled not to eat beans for a month or two."

"You know as well as I do that can't happen. We need to eat, and beans last longer than anything else." Katie smiled as Stanley and Gregory walked back into camp. "What are you boys up to?"

"We were swimming in the creek. Phillip and Mr. Bedwell's boys are still there. I'm sure they'll be back in a minute."

Katie frowned. "I wish you boys hadn't left your brother in the creek."

George spoke up then. "My boys are strong swimmers. Phillip will be fine."

"All right. I'll stop worrying then." It felt strange to Katie to trust George's sons to keep hers safe, but there was no alternative unless she wanted to run down to the river herself. Besides, their children had all taken to looking out for one another.

Chapter Four

Sunday, June 28th, 1852

I don't know what it is about spending time with Katie Gabriel, but I find myself wanting to help others. It always takes me by surprise when I agree to do something nice for someone else when she asks. I guess what it really boils down to is I would do anything for Katie. Anything.

I shot a buffalo today, and in my weakened condition, I couldn't even help bring the animal back to camp. Instead, I had to sit on a rock and rest while some of the younger men of the company brought it to Katie. I did make certain that it would go straight to Katie instead of to my camp.

It felt good to be able to contribute a great beast like that to our food supply. Oh, like Katie always does, she shared it with the other families in camp, but even that didn't bother me. Do I wish she'd kept it for us to use? I'm not even certain.

I'm glad we had a day of rest today because I need it to get stronger. The meat should help me feel like I can do more as well.

Life has taken some strange turns since I jumped in the river to help Anna Gabriel. The child is strong and healthy, and I will be again soon. I'm determined.

Katie Gabriel is a good marriage prospect, and I'm going to make certain she's mine before another man catches her eye. There's just something about her that makes me want to be better. If I can be my best self with Katie around, then she needs to always be by my side. It's only logical.

George sat on a rock at Katie's campfire, and watched as she cooked their supper. The children were all off playing, but they would be back for supper soon. "Are you going to make biscuits to go with our meal?" he asked.

Katie frowned. "I thought about it, because they would be delicious with the roast, but I'm certain I should save the flour for a time when there's no meat to be found."

George frowned. "You know I have plenty of supplies, and we'll be in Fort Bridger within a week or two. We should be able to trade for more flour while we're there."

She smiled at him. "You're just trying to make it okay for us to have a huge meal tonight."

He laughed softly. "I think it would help me grow stronger. And think of all the boys. They'll be able to eat their fill. It's so rare right now that we're able to really eat, I think it would be wonderful if you made biscuits."

Her face softened. "All right. I'll make biscuits." Katie wasn't certain what it was about the man. She'd seen him order everyone else in camp around many times, but he had only shown *her* kindness. Well, that wasn't completely true. When she'd first taken to being a nursemaid for him, he'd yelled at her repeatedly. Even before he'd been able to yell, his whispers had felt like yells. Maybe the man truly was changing. With the help of the Lord, perhaps he would continue to change.

"Thank you. I won't pester you for dessert, but..."

Katie pursed her lips. "Biscuits or dessert? Your choice."

"I'll take the biscuits, but if you think about it, we're having a guest at our fire tonight, and it would be nice if we had a dessert as well to share with her."

"I'm certain she'll be happy enough that I'm cooking for her that she won't mind not having a dessert at all." Katie wasn't going to budge on her decision to make one or the other, no matter how much cajoling George did.

George sighed, but he didn't seem to really mind. Instead, he watched her. She wasn't certain why he watched her so closely. She certainly wasn't a pretty young girl any longer. She'd married Ned when she was only sixteen, and she'd given birth to Stanley at seventeen. Turning thirty on her next birthday made her feel downright old.

As she mixed up the ingredients for biscuits, she thought about Ned and how he would feel that she'd formed such a close friendship—she wasn't even certain friendship was the right word—with another man so soon after his death. She could only hope he'd be pleased that she'd found someone who would provide meat for her and the children.

When the meal had finished cooking, she raised her right hand, and she could see little Anna rushing across the circle of wagons to her. She also caught Jane's eye, and the other women nodded, picking up her Dutch oven and carrying it toward Katie's fire.

The boys came as well, and soon they were all gathered, simply waiting for Jane to finish her trek to them. She nudged Phillip. "Run and carry that pot for Mrs. Davies."

Phillip was an obedient child and didn't have to be told twice. He ran toward the young woman and took the pot from her. Katie could hear his voice as he said, "Please allow me to carry this for you, Mrs. Davies."

Jane nodded and smiled. "Thank you for your kindness."

When they reached camp, Katie smiled. "Children, I'm not certain if you've met Mrs. Davies yet. Her husband died a few days ago, and she's going to be eating with us."

George immediately said, "I'm sorry for your loss, Mrs. Davies. It seems we've all lost our life partners on this trek."

Mrs. Davies seemed startled by the kind words. "Thank you, Mr. Bedwell."

"Starting tomorrow, my older boy, Harvey, will drive your wagon for you," George said. "There's no need for you to do so much work in your condition. Walking with the other women is more than enough."

"Thank you!" Jane looked over at Katie. "You did say you might be able to help with the driving. I appreciate you arranging things for me."

Katie smiled. "No woman should have to drive oxen twenty miles per day when she's expecting. George can drive again, and Harvey has experience."

It was the first Harvey had heard of his new task, but he simply nodded his agreement. "I'll be happy to drive for you, Mrs. Davies."

Katie realized that George's boys had become much kinder in the past couple of weeks as well. It was strange that it had only taken a kind influence in their lives for them to leave behind a lifetime of anger. Hopefully, it would continue that way.

Jane smiled and nodded, and it looked as if the smile reached her eyes for the first time since Katie had begun talking to her at the creek that morning. It was good though. Learning to smile and laugh again had been the two hardest things for Katie after Ned had passed.

George offered to bless their meal, much to Katie's amazement, and his prayer was a good one. She'd worried about letting George and his boys pray aloud for their meals because she hadn't known what would come out of their mouths, but now the worry was gone.

She dished up food for everyone, adding two biscuits to each person's plate. When she handed Jane her plate, Jane said, "Thank you for the meal, Katie. I brought dessert for us all to share."

Katie smiled, shaking her head. "I'm sure everyone will be very happy with that."

George grinned at her, knowing she was thinking of the discussion they'd had just minutes before about having dessert and biscuits all in the same meal. If her mind was on him, George found he was happy. A plan was formulating in his mind to keep her with him forever.

As they all ate the meal, Katie thanked George for shooting the buffalo for them. "It's so nice to have fresh meat for our supper. Thank you, George."

He nodded, but she could tell he was pleased with her recognizing his work.

As soon as everyone had eaten their fill, Jane opened the Dutch oven she'd brought from her own wagon. "I made an apple cinnamon cake. It was my husband's favorite thing I cooked, and he'd ask me to make it every night." Her voice sounded far away as she spoke, but Katie understood. She was mourning her husband, even as she cooked his favorite cake. She wouldn't be able to do anything without thinking of her husband for a while, but gradually, she'd learn to live her own life again.

"Thank you for letting us try it. I'll have to get your recipe." Katie had never attempted an apple cinnamon cake. She made cobblers and pies, but not as many cakes as some women did. "I'll share my recipe for cobbler if you'd like."

"I would adore that. Thank you." Jane seemed like she'd come back from her short trip to visit her deceased husband.

All of the children raved about the cake, the Bedwell boys taking their cue from her children. It seemed no one had attempted to teach the boys manners, but they were picking them up a little at a time. She was pleased that her children were able to teach the manners she'd ingrained in them to the Bedwells.

Jane insisted on staying and helping Katie with the dishes.

"But Anna helps with the dishes. You should go rest. I cannot imagine being on the trail and expecting," Katie said. She really didn't think the other woman should have to help with the dishes for the large group of people she cooked for every night.

Jane shook her head. "I will either help with the dishes, or I'll need to refuse any further invitations to eat with you."

Katie sighed. "All right. Anna, thank Mrs. Davies, and then you may go and find your friends."

Anna smiled. "Thank you, Mrs. Davies."

Jane smiled at Anna. "Thank you for letting me eat supper with you."

"You're welcome!" Anna ran off then to play with her friends while the two women did the dishes.

Katie washed and Jane wiped the dishes dry. "I hope you'll eat supper with us every evening," Katie said. "Stanley drives for me, so I'm perfectly capable of adding one more person, but I will probably need a bit of your food stores."

"I'd like that a lot. Thank you, Katie."

"What's one more when I already cook for a large group?" Katie smiled at her new friend, thankful that she was accepting her offers of help.

After the dishes were finished and stowed back in the wagon, Jane went back to her camp. Instead of walking, Katie sat down on one of the rocks beside the fire. All of the children had gone their separate ways, but George remained.

"I was thinking about something," George said softly.

"Oh?" Katie's mind was on the following day when they would be back to walking their twenty miles per day. It wasn't yet the fourth of July, and they were well past the halfway mark. Unless there was an extremely early winter, they would be able to make it to their new homes before the snows, and that would make everything so much easier.

"I think we should get married," George said softly.

Katie stared at him, wondering if somehow one of her children had talked to him about it. "I'm not so sure..."

"Is it my temper you're worried about?" he asked.

She nodded. "I can't risk someone mistreating my children. Ned never yelled at them, and I don't think anyone should start yelling at them now. I can't risk that." It was hard to admit what the problem was, but she needed to be honest with him if they were discussing something as important as marriage.

George sighed. "What if I proved to you that I won't yell at the children?"

"How could you prove that?"

"If I make it until Friday without once yelling at the children, would that convince you?"

"Make it two weeks," she said softly. She wanted to tell him that he had to not yell at them before they reached Oregon City, but she knew that would be asking too much to have him wait that long. She did wish she had someone to lean on who would help her make a living.

He frowned. "Let's say through Monday, and if I do well, we get married Tuesday after the wagons have stopped rolling for the day."

Katie considered what he was asking. She couldn't imagine lying with a man other than her Ned. "I wouldn't want to have marital relations for a while. I haven't stopped mourning my Ned."

"I agree." George wanted to say that he hadn't stopped mourning Patience, but he had to wonder if he'd ever truly mourned Patience. Yes, she was the mother of his children, but his father had told him to marry her when his friend, her father, had died, leaving her an orphan at sixteen. She simply wasn't bold enough to be married to a man like him, and he wasn't sure he'd ever felt love for her...or her for him.

"If you can make it to a week from tomorrow without yelling at my children or me, then I will marry you." Katie hoped she was doing the right thing by even considering marrying the man, but she had to do what was best for the children.

"I think we'd still need to keep both wagons. Even with our diminished food supply, there wouldn't be room for all the food we would need in just one."

Katie nodded. "We really should have brought two wagons for the amount of food we needed with the four children, but we didn't have the money for another wagon and six more oxen. I have my Bible and one book that Phillip begged me to bring, but those are our only possessions we brought beyond what we needed for the trail." Her Phillip loved to read, and she couldn't leave his book behind, even if it meant that she couldn't bring along many of the things she had. Other than the Bible that was her most treasured possession, she didn't need anything else. Not even the cradle her husband had made for their babies to sleep in, though she'd wept over it as they sold it to a young couple expecting their first child. It had felt like she was losing a piece of herself.

Her Bible was more important though. It had belonged to her father's grandmother, and their entire family was listed in it, generation after generation. There wasn't a keepsake more important to Katie.

George nodded. "Two would have been good, but if you didn't bring many keepsakes, then it should have worked."

She nodded. "Ned was very careful about what we brought with us."

Phillip ran into camp then. "Mama! Look what I found!" He held up a book. "It was just sitting there on a rock. May I keep it and take it to Oregon with us?"

Katie frowned. "You know I told you only one book. You must decide if you want the new one, or the one you brought from home."

Phillip looked as if he'd cry for a moment, but he straightened his shoulders. "I'll put my old book on the rock where I found this one, and perhaps another child will pick it up and they can put the book they have there."

She loved the solution. "I think that's a wonderful idea. Someone else would love to read your book."

Phillip threw his arms around her. "Thank you, Mama. I can't wait to start reading."

"Promise me you won't read while we're walking again." She shook her head, looking at George. "He tripped over a rock, and if it hadn't been for Stanley's quick thinking, we'd have lost him. He landed right next to a rattlesnake, but Stanley found a rock and bashed it over the head."

George smiled at that. "Stanley is an impressive young man." He could easily see that her Stanley at thirteen could do anything his fifteen-year-old son, Harvey, could do. It was a testament to his parents that he was so able. George could see how her style of "soft parenting" had worked, and he was truly impressed by it.

Katie smiled at him, one of her rare smiles that lit up her whole face and made him feel as if he was in the presence of the sun. "Thank you." The compliment was for Stanley of course, but she knew her son was the way he was because of her and Ned's teachings.

Phillip looked back and forth between the adults. "I'm going to get my book and take it back to the rock," he said.

"That sounds like a good idea. I want you back in camp by sundown, so we can all sleep."

"Yes, Mama!" He ran back toward the rock where he'd found the book, and Katie smiled.

"My mother couldn't read, but she made sure I could. I taught my three boys, and when we reach Oregon, I'll work on teaching Anna. I hate that my mother couldn't even read the Bible and had to rely on my sisters and me."

George shrugged. "I never really thought a woman needed to know how to read. Patience could, and she spent all of her time reading, and left the maid to do the housework, cook, and take care of the boys."

Katie frowned. "I would never suggest a woman should read and not take care of her responsibilities. I read my Bible in the evenings, after all my chores are done."

"I know you would never shirk your duties, Katie. I've seen you do everything you could to care for me, while still feeding your children and mine. You are truly a remarkable woman."

"Thank you." Katie wasn't sure why his compliment made her feel so good about herself, but it did. Obviously, his wife hadn't been willing to do much outside of reading, and it made her understand his attitude about the mother of his boys so much better than anything else ever would.

George got to his feet. "Walking so much today has tired me out more than it should have. I'm going to head to bed." He was ten feet out of camp before he turned back to Katie. "Thank you for considering my offer." And then he was gone.

Katie couldn't help but wonder if considering it was the right thing, because her children had to come first. No matter what. And having a father was the right thing for her babies.

Chapter Five

Monday, June 29th, 1852

To my surprise, George Bedwell, the man who saved Anna has asked me to be his wife. I'm not sure I trust him because of his temper, but he promised me he is a changed man. If he hasn't yelled at anyone by a week from today, I will be forced to believe he can hold his temper in check, and I will marry him. If not, he will never be a father-figure to my children. They are too precious to me.

I've made friends with the most recent widow of the company. Her name is Jane Davies, and she'll be eating with us each evening. She is insisting on helping with the dishes, which I appreciate, but the woman is in the family way, and I'd rather she rests when she can. George's older boy, Harvey, will be driving her wagon from now on. I think that will remove at least part of her burden.

It was bad enough for me when I lost my Ned, but I cannot imagine what it would be like if I'd been expecting. This trail...I understand why Ned wanted us to move to the west. We stand to gain a great deal financially because of the free government land, but it is the most difficult thing I've ever done. I would rather go through childbirth than walk this trail, but walking is what I do every day. My children will benefit from it, but that doesn't mean it doesn't weigh heavily on me that they are in danger as am I.

We will be moving again today, and I'm pleased that Mrs. Davies will be walking along with the other women again.

She had been married less than a month when she and her husband began this journey, and she kept to herself mostly. She and her husband spent every spare minute together—as newlyweds do—and she didn't take the time to get to know the other women, the people who can help her from here on out. The men don't think to look out for others. They simply make certain their families are safe. We women—we work hard to take care of each other.

As the oxen were hitched to their respective wagons Monday morning, Katie found Jane and asked if she would like to walk with her. When the other woman agreed, Katie introduced her to the friends she'd made along the way—Hannah, Mary, Margaret, Betty, Penelope, and Trudie. All of the women were happy to accept her as their friend.

The group tended to try to keep each other occupied as they walked, and there was much revelry and laughter as they plodded along toward the elephant—Oregon. It seemed each day that they felt further and further away from their destination, but not one of them was willing to turn around and go back. They'd come too far.

As they walked, Betty looked over at Katie. "I see that you're spending a lot of time with the former captain. Are you sure it's safe to have him around your children?" The look of concern on Betty's face was real, and Katie knew Betty had her own difficulties with George.

Katie nodded. "He's...different now. He's much calmer and doesn't yell nearly as much." She took a deep breath. "He asked me to marry him last night." She hadn't planned to tell anyone about the offer, but it felt right to get it out in the open.

Betty gasped. "You're not considering it, are you?" Her eyes were wide, and it was obvious by her face that she had no hope for a marriage between the two of them.

"I am. My children need a father, and he has been nothing but kind." Not for the past few days anyway. "I will give him my answer in a week. He's given me some time to consider." Katie didn't want the other women to know the arrangement she'd made with George because she was certain they wouldn't understand. No one saw George quite the way she did. Besides, they didn't need to know she was asking him to prove he could hold his temper in check.

Trudie shook her head. "Oh, Katie. I saw the way he talked to you when I sat with him while you went to church with the children. Even his boys were hiding from him." The pity in Trudie's eyes made Katie want to explain how different he was, but she had a feeling the other women wouldn't understand.

Katie sighed. "I know. It's different now that he's not an invalid though. He thanks me for every meal, and believe it or not, his boys do as well. It's rather remarkable when you think about the manners they didn't display before. His boys have even taken my older two sons under their wings, and they help them learn to be better hunters. I appreciate all he and his boys have done for my family. And George risked his own life to save my Anna. How could I think poorly of them, knowing that?"

Hannah nodded at Katie. "I understand. God is good, and if people make a real change, he forgives. We should forgive as well." Hannah—the pastor's wife—had changed a lot on the trail as well. Katie couldn't help but admire the other woman, though she was much younger than Katie.

Margaret shrugged. "If you feel like he won't harm you or your children, and it seems like the right decision, you should marry him. Our opinions don't matter at all. Only yours."

Katie smiled. "Thank you for saying that, Margaret." It felt good to know someone understood her. If anyone would, it would be Margaret, who had recently married for the second time. Her two girls were the most important thing to her, and Katie respected that.

The three Henderson children walked past then. Their mother had been the first casualty of the journey, and their father drove all day. At first, they'd walked with Hannah and Mary, but now they tended to just plod along on their own every day.

The oldest Henderson child, Natalie, smiled as they moved past the group of women. "Hello, Mrs. Scott."

Hannah smiled. "How are you three today?"

"We're good. I made supper last night and no one died from eating it!" Natalie couldn't be older than ten, and Katie bit back the invitation to allow the other family to eat with them. She was already cooking for nine people. It wouldn't be smart to add four more.

"If you need help cooking, you can always ask me," Katie offered.

"Thank you, Mrs. Gabriel. I might stop by sometime." Natalie didn't seem overly excited at the offer though. She looked at Katie's boot. "You need your boot fixed. You should talk to my pa. He's a cobbler."

Katie hadn't realized they had a cobbler in their group. "I will do that!" Her right foot had been hurting since a hole had developed in the side. She would be certain to go to Mr. Henderson the next time they were in camp for a while. It would be good to perhaps cook a meal and trade it for mending the boot she wore. It was her second pair of shoes she'd worn out on this walk. If he could fix just one of them, maybe she could save the third pair she'd brought for after their arrival in Oregon.

"Pa would just tell you he'd work in exchange. Make us a meal, and he'll happily fix your boot. And then I won't have to cook for a night. Everyone would win!"

Katie laughed. "I'll be sure to do that."

As the children walked away, the topic turned to the book Phillip had found. "On a rock beside the creek, Phillip—my reader—found a book someone had left behind. I made him choose between the book he found and the one he'd brought with him, and he chose the new book. He left the other book on the same rock he'd found the new book on. I hope another child will find the book and enjoy it as much as Phillip has."

Betty, who read more books than anyone else, grinned. "I think that's wonderful. It's like there's a book exchange happening out here in the middle of nowhere. A book train if you will."

Katie nodded. "You should have seen how excited Phillip was to have a new book to read along the way. He's read the other one so many times, I think he's memorized it." She shook her head. "I'd complain about his reading all day if he didn't do the chores I give him and play with the other children some, but he does those things, so I'm just proud of him for reading. Why wouldn't I be?"

Jane stopped for a moment, her hand going to her abdomen. "I think the babe is moving," she said.

"How far along do you think you are?" Margaret asked.

"Maybe eight weeks?" Jane said.

"It's probably not the baby moving just yet," Katie said. "I had pains and strange sensations in my stomach the entire time I carried all four of mine."

Margaret nodded. "Me too."

Mary looked at Jane. "If you think there's a problem, I'll fetch my ma. She's a midwife." Mary had obviously seen enough trouble with pregnancies she was immediately concerned.

Jane shook her head. "I don't think that's necessary. I'm sure Margaret and Katie are right. The babe is just making its presence known."

"If it keeps up, you just let my ma know about it, and she'll know what to do."

Katie smiled at her friend, who had begun walking again. "I'm making stew for supper tonight with the leftover from our buffalo roast yesterday."

Jane smiled. "That sounds lovely." Her eyes were distant again, though, and Katie knew she was thinking of the husband she'd left behind. They'd buried him right on the trail for the rest of the company to roll over, so his dirt would be packed down, and he wouldn't be found by wolves, or grave robbed by Indians.

"Don't feel like you always need to provide a dessert, though," Katie said. "I don't want my children to think a meal isn't complete without a sweet to finish it off."

Mary shook her head. "I know my younger brothers and sisters think that. They're all spoiled though."

Hannah smiled. "I wouldn't call your siblings spoiled." Hannah tried to never speak poorly of anyone.

"You don't know them like *I* do!"

When they stopped for their noon meal, Katie made certain to let Jane know she was invited to join them. "It will just be some of last night's meal, but it was good the first time, so should be just as good the second."

"I don't think that's a good idea. I'll just eat some hard tack. My stomach doesn't want me to eat anything until suppertime."

Katie nodded, understanding. "Get some rest while we are stopped then. No need for you to wear yourself out when you don't feel like you can eat anyway." She was glad Jane knew how to get around the queasiness already, and Katie said a silent prayer that Jane would know when it was important to talk to a midwife or doctor.

When they'd stopped, Katie quickly got out their food from the night before, and she served it up onto everyone's plates. They only stopped for two hours for the noon meal, and it was good if everyone could sleep for an hour of that. There was no need to start a fire to warm up the food. They'd just eat it cold.

While Katie prepared the meal for the two families, she was well-aware of the other activity in the camp. The oxen were unhitched and allowed to rest; a fresh pair would be put on each wagon for the afternoon drive. Children gathered with their families, and older children helped with the livestock.

When everyone was together at the back of her wagon, Phillip said the prayer. She hadn't yet asked either of George's boys to pray, unsure what type of church upbringing they'd had. She would have to let one of them pray soon, though, so they wouldn't feel slighted.

As they ate, they all talked about what they'd seen that day. There they were, between two major milestones of the trip. They had passed Independence Rock, where they'd carved their names and they were yet to make it to Fort Bridger. Katie wanted to make sure her letter to her family was ready to mail before they reached Fort Bridger, but every time she put pen to paper, something happened that required her attention.

They'd been in Oregon Territory for a while, but no one had seen the place they wanted to spend the rest of their lives. This area was flat with prairie grasses and no real trees. They wanted a place that had access to fresh water, and some trees would be nice. Trees were needed for building, though they'd certainly found a way around burning trees as firewood.

When they'd first had to use buffalo manure to feed their fires, Katie had worried the smell would be overwhelming and the chips would burn too quickly. Instead, the fuel hadn't had a foul odor and the manure had burned as long as a log of wood. It was truly a wonderful alternative fuel.

Stanley looked extremely tired to Katie, and she was suddenly worried that something had made him sick. "Are you feeling all right, Stanley?" she asked.

Stanley nodded. "I didn't sleep well last night. I'm not sure why, but I'm awful tired today."

Katie frowned, wishing she knew what to do. "I can drive this afternoon, and you can ride in the back of the wagon." She wasn't comfortable driving the oxen, but it didn't seem as if she had a choice. Her son's health was more important than her discomfort.

George shook his head. "Albert will drive your wagon this afternoon. There's no need for you to drive."

Katie bit her lip, hating the idea of taking even more help, but she realized that if their families were to merge into one, she would have to get used to relying on George and his sons. "I would appreciate that if you don't mind." She looked over at Stanley. "I want you to nap until we leave this afternoon. Perhaps you'll feel up to walking."

Stanley nodded. "I'm sorry, Ma. I'm trying to do my share." He looked disappointed in himself, but she'd been worried about him for days. He was trying to do too much as the "man of the family."

"You've done more than your share since your pa fell sick. You deserve an afternoon of riding instead of walking."

Stanley nodded, finishing the last two bites of his noon meal, and climbing under the wagon to sleep. Katie was pleased to see how quickly he'd obeyed, but she was still a bit worried about him. She'd leaned on him for a good long while, and he deserved rest.

George frowned at Katie. "Do you think he's getting sick?"

Katie shrugged. "Perhaps. I certainly hope not." She looked at her son, lying there looking so small under the wagon. "I know he hasn't had anything to drink except coffee. If he didn't sleep last night, then it makes sense that he's tired today."

"I suppose it does."

Anna moved close to her mother and wrapped her arms around her. "Will Stanley be all right?"

"Of course, he will!" Katie said, saying a silent prayer she was right. She hadn't thought she'd lose Ned either, but losing Stanley as well? She was certain her heart would shatter into a million pieces, and there would be no reason for her to even try to continue on. "Go and lie down in the back of the wagon. You need your sleep as well."

Anna grumbled a little, claiming she was too old for naps, but then she spotted her brother and stopped immediately. "Yes, Mama."

Katie was aware of George's gaze on her, but she said nothing else as she sat there, engrossed in prayer until their noon break was over.

Stanley slept in the back of the wagon until they reached their stopping point for the day—yet another campsite without fresh water. They'd all filled their barrels the night before, though, so it would all be fine.

She made stew for supper that night, and Stanley ate more than his share. Katie felt better watching how strong his appetite was. Jane looked at Katie with a smile. "He's got his appetite back."

Katie nodded. "Are you feeling better this evening, Stanley?"

Stanley nodded. "I'm sorry if I worried you, Ma. I should have rested more yesterday."

"As long as you're all right, I have nothing to complain about. You do a man's work every day, and your pa would be so proud of you."

Stanley's chest seemed to grow three inches at the compliment. "I miss him every day."

Katie nodded. "I do too."

After the supper dishes were washed—by Jane and Anna—everyone went in their own direction. Katie invited Jane to stay at her campfire, but the other woman told her she was too tired. The fatigue on her face was clear.

So, George and Katie sat together at the fire, listening to the sounds of the others in the camp around them. "Are you still worried about Stanley?" George finally asked.

Katie sighed. "I am. I can see he's doing better than he was earlier, but it's a mother's job to worry about her children. I take that job very seriously."

George chuckled. "I can ask the doctor to look at him if it would make you feel better."

"Not at all," Katie said. She knew there was no reason to bother the doctor except to make *her* feel better, and that's not why a doctor should look at a patient—for their mother to stop worrying. "How was the drive for you today? You don't look as tired as you did on Saturday evening."

"I think it was easier today. Every day seems to get a little easier. I was sure I'd have to be left at the side of the trail with my boys going on without me, but thanks to you, that didn't have to happen. Have I told you how much I appreciate the way you took care of me?"

"You mean you didn't mean it when you kept yelling at me when I made you eat when you didn't want to?" she asked, smiling.

"You know I didn't." He shook his head. "I don't know why my temper has always been so bad." But George did know. There was just no way he wanted to admit it to her. His father had been a drinker, and he'd been mean when he'd gotten into his cups. George had simply followed his father's example in marriage and parenting. He'd thought he was doing the best thing but watching Katie had taught him better. Her children obeyed because they loved and respected her. It had nothing to do with fear.

"You're getting better," Katie told him. "That's the important thing."

"I try every day. I've started praying when I wake up that I'll be able to keep my temper in check."

"I had some temper issues when I was a girl. My mother had me memorize Galatians 5:22-23. Then when I started to get angry, she'd have me list the fruits of the spirit in my head. It has always worked for me."

"I'll look that up," George said with a smile. "I cannot imagine you losing your temper."

"I think you're the only person who has seen me lose it since I was six or seven. You made me want to throw rocks at your head...but I couldn't because you saved my little girl."

"I guess I wasn't a very good patient."

She shrugged. "Not particularly. I think anyone would have trouble being a patient under those circumstances though. Have I told you how very happy I am that you survived?"

"No, but I'm glad." He got to his feet. "I'm going to go turn in. The day starts earlier every day it seems."

"Goodnight, George," she said softly.

As she watched him go, she had a little talk with Ned in her mind.

"I miss you so much, but if George can keep his word and not yell at the children for a full week, I will marry him. He would be a good provider for me and our children. I don't believe I could ever love him as I love you, but he's a changed man from what I can see, and he deserves a chance at happiness. He's always been kind to me when he wasn't ill. Hopefully, that will continue. Please forgive me if I do marry so soon. It would make it so much easier to reach Oregon City. All of the weight would no longer be on my shoulders." She rubbed the back of her neck, wishing it was Ned's hands rubbing away the tension of the day. "Goodnight, my love."

Chapter Six

Friday, July 2nd, 1852

This has been a very long week, but I feel myself growing stronger every day. We have been traveling along the Green River since Tuesday, and it feels safer to be close to water again—despite my experience with almost drowning in the North Platte.

We have made good time this week, going from Three Crossings to the point where we will arrive at Fort Bridger by late Monday. The days are long, but thankfully, the new captains have kept up my pace, and we still travel twenty miles most days.

There was a sudden storm this afternoon, and we all stayed in our wagons, not wanting to risk being hit by the thunder or lightning. I have a feeling we won't be able to travel tomorrow. If it was up to me, I would say we don't travel tomorrow but we travel Sunday instead, but I know the feelings of the company in general by now, and I know they won't move on the Sabbath.

I have managed to keep my temper since Sunday. I haven't even felt the anger rising within me but once, and that was when Harvey complained that he needed a day off from driving because his arms were getting tired. Thankfully, I remembered what Katie had suggested, and I recited the fruits of the spirit, and to my surprise, they worked, and my anger went away quickly. I didn't let Harvey shirk his job of driving for Mrs.

Davies, though. He needs to learn to do a hard day of work when necessary.

I look forward to getting to Fort Bridger, where we may mail letters and, more importantly, trade for new supplies. We should be able to replenish our flour, sugar, and cornmeal, as well as bacon. There won't be enough for everyone, but I know that I have the gold coins needed to purchase what my family needs, as well as purchasing what Katie's family needs.

Katie has not yet agreed to marry me, but we will discuss our plans again on Monday evening. I hope she will agree. Every day my feelings for her grow. I feel for her like I should have felt for Patience when we married, but I never did. I believe Katie is the love of my life, and I will always treat her as such.

Saturday evening had them all eating cold meals because it was too wet to start fires. Katie handed out the buffalo jerky she'd dried the week before with the other women and gave everyone pieces of hard tack. She knew her children hated hard tack, but it was food. If they sucked on the hard cracker for long enough, it would get soft, and they would have nourishment from it.

Anna looked like she wanted to cry as she was handed the hard tack, but she looked into Katie's face, and she managed to school her face into a smile. "Thank you for feeding us when it's difficult."

Katie was proud of her girl. "We do what we must. Tomorrow we'll eat better. We have fresh rainwater, and now we're all clean. That's helpful."

George and his sons ate from their own stores, having the same supplies as Katie had. Since nothing needed to be cooked, there was no reason to eat with her family. Katie felt strange having only her own children to feed for the first time in a long while.

"Do you think we'll leave camp tomorrow?" Stanley asked.

Katie shook her head. "The ground is too wet. I believe we'll have to stay here until Monday."

Phillip's eyes lit up. "Three whole nights in one place? That will be nice!"

Gregory, who was two years older than Phillip, and saw himself as his brother's teacher, said, "You won't think it's nice if we get stuck in a snowstorm on our way to Oregon City."

Katie frowned at Gregory. "We left early enough that shouldn't happen. Especially with as rigid as we've been about going twenty miles per day six days per week. We should have our claims made long before winter sets in." She hoped so at least. She'd heard they could have an early violent winter starting in September. She prayed that wouldn't be the case.

While it was just her family, she brought up George and his boys. "Has Mr. Bedwell yelled at any of you lately?"

Anna shook her head. "He's never yelled at me, Mama."

Phillip thought long and hard. "Not since he got better."

"He yelled at me after he saved Anna, but not after he started walking again," Stanley said.

Gregory shrugged. "I think he only yelled at me once, and that was before Anna even fell in the water."

Katie nodded. "He's asked me to marry him. How would you children feel about that?"

They all exchanged looks with each other. Finally, Stanley spoke for all of them. "I think it would be fine, and you wouldn't have to worry so much."

Katie smiled. "You need to stop worrying about me, Stanley. It would be nice not to have all decisions on me, and I would like to have someone to share my difficulties with, but I won't marry someone who you feel would mistreat you."

"I don't think he would," Gregory said. "He looks at you like you're a giant piece of cake, and he wants to eat you."

Katie gasped at her son's words. "No, he doesn't!"

Stanley nodded. "He does whenever you're not looking. I think he loves you. And we really like Harvey and Albert. They've become good friends to us, and they're always looking out for us."

"So, you think I should marry him?" Including all her children in her question, she waited to see if any of them had an objection. A small part of her hoped one of them would, so she wouldn't have to make the difficult decision on her own.

All four of her children nodded. "I think it would make your life a lot easier," Stanley said. "Then you have someone to provide for you, and you don't have to start a ranch with just four children to help you."

Katie took a deep breath and nodded. "All right. I'll keep praying about it, and we'll see what happens."

They spread a large piece of oil cloth on the ground that the five of them could sleep on, but they didn't bother with their tent that night, as they rarely did anyway. As long as they could sleep on a dry surface, Katie was sure they'd be fine.

While the children went to sleep, Katie had another quick talk with Ned. *The children all want me to marry George. I was rather hoping one of them would have an objection to the marriage, so I wouldn't have to make the decision about whether or not I should marry him so soon after your death. I guess the full decision lies with me now. I've been praying about it, and I feel like it would be best for me and the children, but at the same time, I feel like I would be betraying you. How can I marry another man so soon after you have died? It doesn't feel right, but I know that I will do better if I have someone to lean on. Oh, Ned, will you ever be able to forgive me if I marry the man? I certainly hope so.*

She lay awake for a long while thinking about Ned and what it would be like to marry the former captain. He was an attractive man, and she felt as if a marriage to him would be good for the family. But the fact that she found him attractive made it worse in her mind. What if she developed real feelings toward the man? Ned was the love of her life, not George Bedwell.

She sighed and finally rolled to her side, praying for sleep. She had to quit tormenting herself over this decision and let things rest as they were. If George didn't lose his temper with one of the children before Monday evening, she would marry him Tuesday. Plain and simple. Otherwise, she'd be going back on her word.

She couldn't do that and feel like she was setting the right example for her children. No, if George didn't yell, she'd be his wife on Tuesday evening. No matter how much the other women tried to tell her it wasn't a good idea. They hadn't seen the same George she had.

Yes, he was a man with a temper, but he was also gentle and loving with her. And he'd learned to be gentle with the children. She even believed he could lead their group to Oregon City now, if he was given the chance again, but she didn't see that happening.

*****

The company had to stay in place on Saturday because the mud was severe. There was no way the wagons could make it through. The wheels would be stuck in the mud so badly that they would have a hard time moving when they were ready, so it was best to stay.

The men hunted, and the women washed clothes and enjoyed their day of rest. Mrs. Mitchell sat weaving a colorful rug with old scraps of cloth and a wagon wheel. Margaret Prewitt filled her tub and sold baths for five cents each. It was a true day of rest for most of the women.

The men came back to camp empty-handed. "The storm must have chased the game off," George told Katie. "I think we're stuck with beans for supper tonight."

Katie sighed. "I'll make biscuits and gravy with chunks of the jerky in it. It's not like fresh meat, but better than beans."

He nodded. "I think that would make all of the children happy...and this man as well. I grow tired of those beans."

"Do you think we'll be able to trade for some supplies at Fort Bridger? I could use some more flour and potatoes for certain. I've heard there are Indians camped near the fort, and they tend to trade food for other things."

George nodded. "We should be able to get what we need. We may even be able to trade for some fresh meat, which would be really nice."

Katie nodded. "That would be *wonderful*." They'd been blessed with a lot of fresh meat lately, and she hoped the blessings continued. She always felt like she'd done the right thing by her children when she served them a meal with fresh meat.

"Last time I came through here, the Indians all had salmon, and they'd take anything brightly colored for it. If you have a pretty hat or a quilt you've made, they'd give you almost anything for it."

"I might trade a shirt of Ned's. I found some red fabric on sale, and I made him a shirt, but he always hated it. It's had little wear, and perhaps the Indians would like that for some corn or potatoes." She didn't want to trade for fresh meat, because it wouldn't last long anyway.

While she made supper, George sat beside her fire on the ground. They hadn't stopped at a normal stopping point for travelers because they had to stop at a sudden storm. There were no rocks set around campfires or seats of any kind that had been set up. Instead, they were eating all their meals on the ground.

Anna hurried to her mother, well before she was expected for supper, and she gave her a fistful of wildflowers she'd picked. "Thank you!" Katie told her daughter. "They're beautiful!"

As Anna skipped away back to her friends, Katie held up the bright red flowers. "What are these?" she asked. George knew a great deal more about the vegetation in the areas they were traveling than she did.

"That's Indian paintbrush," he told her. "They're awful pretty." He wished he'd thought to pick her some flowers himself, but her daughter had beaten him to it.

Katie brought them to her nose and sniffed them. "I love it when she thinks to do little things like that for me. Phillip is the only boy who brings me flowers, and he won't do it if anyone is looking. He doesn't want anyone calling him a Nancy boy."

George smiled. "My boys would definitely call him that if they saw him bringing you flowers. I'll let them know that they shouldn't use that expression anymore. Although, I'm afraid they learned it from me."

Katie shook her head, finding a tin cup and adding a bit of their water as well as the flowers. "I'm glad you're now teaching them to be kind."

"I...well, I have never seen anyone be kind to women and children. My father wasn't a good example of kindness, and I never learned. I think it's something that you really do need to be taught." He sighed. "Thank you for teaching me how to treat people, Katie."

"Didn't Patience ever suggest you should be kinder to people?"

He shrugged. "I suppose, but I didn't listen to what she said much."

Katie shook her head. "If we marry, you'll have to take my feelings and thoughts into account. You can't treat me like you treated your wife."

"I won't. I have too much respect for you to treat you poorly." He wished he knew the right way to convince her that he would always do his best to treat people with kindness, but he just didn't know what would convince her.

She stood and raised her hand for the children and Jane to come for supper and then started dishing up their meals. "Thank you for trying to get meat for us," she said as she worked.

"You thank me for something I wasn't able to do?" Never had he heard a woman do something like that. Of course, his mother had died when he was a boy, and his father had remarried someone very young who allowed him to boss her around. He wasn't sure if his stepmother had any kind of personality at all, because she was always shying away from his father.

"You tried. I think effort deserves thanks," she said.

Then the children were there, and Gregory said the prayer. All of them took their meals. "I hope you all enjoy this," Katie said. "I didn't want to have to make beans."

Anna squealed and hugged her mother. "Anything is better than beans, Mama. Anything!"

Katie laughed. "Starving is not better than beans," she said for what felt like the hundredth time since they'd left Pennsylvania.

"I reckon not," Phillip said, tucking into his food. "This is good, Mama. Tasty."

"Thank you."

Harvey smiled at Katie. "Thank you for finding a meal we could eat that didn't consist of beans. Sometimes I think if I have to eat one more bean, I may have to cut my tongue out, so I won't taste them."

"I think that would be a bit extreme," Katie responded with a laugh.

"I'm not so sure!" Stanley said dramatically.

After the supper dishes were done, and Katie and George were once again left alone at the fire, George asked a question Katie had been dreading. "How are you feeling about my marriage proposal?"

Katie took a deep breath and a sip of her cold coffee to combat her suddenly dry mouth. "I think I'm willing. Just a couple more days."

"I think I've done well. The only time I wanted to get angry, I listed the fruits of the spirit just like you suggested. I was really surprised when it worked for me."

"That's wonderful! Who were you angry with?"

"Harvey. He thought he should get a day off driving and someone else should do it, but I explained that a man does the work he says he'll do and doesn't shirk. He drove and hasn't complained a lick since."

Katie grinned. "I think that's wonderful. Harvey is a good boy, he just needs a good example to follow, and you've done great becoming that."

George thought of the years he'd used a loud voice and a switch on his boys to get them to do whatever he wanted, and he realized that he could have done everything without half as much anger. "I'm trying my best to be the kind of father I would like them to be someday."

Katie looked at him. "Do you drink spirits, George?"

"I don't. After seeing my father get drunk so many times as a boy, I decided that I had no desire to even try spirits. I haven't tried them even once."

"That's wonderful!" Katie said. "I'm glad you learned from your father's mistakes, and you don't do that."

"Did Ned drink?" he asked.

She shrugged. "He'd drink on occasion, but it was only ever *one* drink, and never at home. He'd stop and have a drink with some of the men on his way home from work, but it was never more than once a month."

"Then he was a man who could handle his liquor. Most men that I've known can't handle it at all."

She tilted her head to one side and studied him. Her father had drunk on occasion as well, but he'd never been inebriated in front of her. Perhaps he'd known a different kind of man than she had.

"What do you want to do once you reach your homestead?" she asked.

He smiled. "I want to have a ranch, but mostly, I want to train horses. It's a childhood dream of mine, and that's why I wanted to head west. The free land will work in my favor, and I'll have plenty of room for cattle and horses."

"It sounds like you're doing the right thing for you then. Ned wanted to have a ranch. It's always been his dream, so when he told me he wanted to head west, I was all for it. I wanted to see his dreams come true. And he instilled those same dreams in my boys, who will carry on his legacy. Stanley made certain I knew he'd start the ranch his father had always wanted." Katie could still see Stanley kneeling beside her dying husband, telling him he would make his father's dream come true, and the ranch would be started in his honor.

Knowing that George would help Stanley to start a ranch, Katie knew marrying him was the right thing. She simply had to tell Ned and pray that George would be good to her children.

Chapter Seven

Sunday, July 4th, 1852

It's our nation's birthday, and we're celebrating by having a church service, and then we will all meet and have one of our dances. No one had room for fireworks—and it was too dangerous to bring them along—so they will not be part of the celebration, but we will celebrate nonetheless.

I am excited to spend the day with my children. Because we had a day without travel yesterday, the laundry is all washed, and I don't have work to do today other than cooking for my family, which I must admit is a never-ending task.

Hopefully, someone will get some game, or the boys will get fish from the river. I would love to be able to feed my family something hearty for our holiday. I have always had a special affinity with our country's birthday because it coincides with my birthday. I am thirty years old today, but I feel a great deal older. I'm a widow with four children. I'm definitely past the first bloom of youth. I don't know if I'll have any more children, though Ned and I hoped for at least one more. Four seems incomplete somehow, but five? That sounds like a family to be proud of.

The former captain has kept his end of the bargain, and he hasn't shown his temper at all since we talked about the possibility of us marrying. I do hope he continues to keep our bargain long after we have married.

The children all agree that they'd like me to marry him. I think Stanley only likes the idea because he knows my life will be easier if everything isn't weighing on my shoulders.

I doubt if any of the children will remember it's my birthday, and though I love to celebrate, I will not run amok announcing it to the other emigrants. No, I'll have a quiet, private birthday, and I'll remember my Ned. It's my first birthday without him, and I will miss him even more today than usual.

Now I must go join my family for our church service, and then I will happily attend our Independence Day celebrations. Happy birthday, United States. And happy birthday to me.

Katie and her children walked toward the area where the pastor had declared they would have church services. It was rare for them to have to sit on the ground because so many companies had come this way before them, many of them adding places to sit to make it easier for themselves and those who came behind them.

She sat with her children and was surprised when George and his boys joined the group, sitting with them. George presented her with a bouquet of flowers as he took his seat on the ground. "Happy birthday," he whispered.

Katie was shocked. "How did you know?"

"Stanley. He wanted to make sure everyone knew to help you have a wonderful holiday and birthday." George smiled at her, and the smile seemed to reach his eyes. Normally, his smiles just changed his face, but when they reached his eyes, she knew they were genuine.

"Thank you," Katie said with a smile, hugging the flowers to her. She hadn't been forgotten, and it warmed her heart to receive the gift of wildflowers.

After the sermon, many crowded around her. She had no idea how many people had been told it was her special day, but people kept calling, "Happy birthday!" to her, and Katie truly felt special.

Supper that night consisted of fresh rainbow trout and fried potatoes. All five boys had headed to the river immediately after their church service, and they hadn't come home empty handed. They'd even cleaned and deboned the fish before giving them to her to cook.

As soon as the supper dishes were cleaned up, they all headed to the area where they'd had church, where they'd all decided to hold their music as well. The band played lively songs, and Katie couldn't quite believe her eyes when George held his hand out to her and asked her to dance.

She got to her feet with his help and went into his arms. It was the first time they'd danced together, and they stood close to one another as they danced the waltz. She knew many considered the dance scandalous, but to her, it was great fun.

The odd young woman, Edna, was waltzing as well, but her partner was invisible. It was very strange to see, but Edna looked happy. Watching her always made Katie feel like she was missing out on something. Everyone should be as free as young Edna.

As they danced, George kept his eyes on hers, and she found herself surprised he was such an accomplished dancer. She couldn't help but wonder who had taught him to dance, but she didn't ask. She was afraid if they started talking, she would miss the beat and step on his toes.

At the end of the song, they all applauded, and George and Katie returned to their spot on the grass where they'd been listening to the band.

As soon as they were seated, Margaret came over with a plate. She handed it to Katie with a smile. "Happy birthday, my friend. I hope you know how much we all love you."

Katie's eyes filled with tears for just a moment as she thought about the one who had loved her more than anyone else. "Thank you. I thought about baking a cake today, but I doubted anyone remembered my birthday."

"Stanley made sure everyone knew. The boy loves you."

"I love him too." Katie looked over at Stanley, who was beaming with pride. She knew he had really thought about her if he remembered to tell people. "I'll return your plate washed in the morning."

"There's no hurry," Margaret said, but Katie knew better. Margaret fed the men and children who had lost their wives and mothers. She needed all the dishes she had and then some.

Phillip asked Anna to dance, and the two of them showed them all how it was done. They bowed and curtseyed to one another and though neither really knew how to dance, they moved along to the music, making everyone smile.

As they watched, Edna came over to stand in front of George and Katie. "I never would have thought anyone would be willing to make the sacrifice of marrying the former captain," Edna said, "but you two just look like you belong together. I know you'll have beautiful babies."

Katie blushed deeply. Even though George had said they could wait to be intimate, it still was embarrassing that Edna would say such a thing with everyone in the entire company right there. Well, everyone but sweet Jane, who had gone to bed straight after supper, as was her habit. Katie was unsure if she went to bed early to mourn her husband or because she was genuinely that tired. Either way, she was glad her friend was doing her best to take care of herself.

Finally, after a stunned silence from everyone, Katie said, "Thank you for giving us your opinion on the matter." What else could she say? She didn't want to hurt the girl's feelings, even if what she said was entirely inappropriate.

After the dance, George escorted Katie back to her wagon. "I hope your birthday was wonderful."

She smiled and nodded. "I truly didn't expect the children to remember. I didn't realize they even knew what the date was, though I guess having our Independence Day celebrations gave it away."

He smiled and nodded. "I don't think Stanley would have remembered if not for the celebration, but I'm glad he did." He leaned down and kissed her cheek. "Sleep well."

Katie stood staring after him as he walked away. It was the first time he'd shown any real affection to her, and it startled her. Surprisingly, her heart was beating faster after the kiss on the cheek, and it didn't take any investigating to realize that she was attracted to him. His beard and his strong arms were very moving to her. Perhaps it wouldn't be terrible to be married to George.

And then she had her talk with Ned. Today was wonderful. It was my first birthday without you, and though I missed you greatly, Stanley made sure everyone in camp knew it was a special day for me, and people were very kind. I believe that I will tell George tomorrow evening that I will marry him. Perhaps it's a mistake, but...It will be what's best for the children, and I think it might be what's best for me.

As Katie fell asleep that night, she felt like she had a real future for the first time since Ned had been injured. Maybe she wasn't marrying someone the other women in camp thought much of, but that didn't matter to her. She could see there was a good person peeking out from under the gruff exterior.

******

They stopped Monday evening just outside of Fort Bridger. As soon as they arrived, the Indians came over to the circle of wagons to try to trade. Katie traded the red shirt that had been Ned's for a fresh deer. The entire deer for a shirt. She felt like she was cheating the savages, but they were willing to trade for the shirt, so it must be fair in their eyes.

She had Stanley drag the deer into camp and hang it from the back of the wagon and begin the long process of butchering the animal.

Thankfully, it was something Ned had taught Stanley to do, so she could simply move out of the way and let her son do the work.

The fort surprised Katie. She'd thought it would be like a small city, but it was really just four cabins, each with a flat roof, surrounded by an eight-foot stockade. The stockade consisted of logs stuck into the ground and standing up, keeping the people inside safe from Indian attack. There were several Indian lodges around the fort. It seemed like a rather bleak place to try to find supplies, but George assured her that there were indeed supplies for trade and purchase.

Each family sent one member into the fort to purchase and trade for what they needed. George went for Katie while she cooked venison steaks for supper. She'd tell him she wanted to marry him in a few short hours, so what did it matter if he purchased her food?

When George came back to camp, he sent the three older boys—Harvey, Albert, and Stanley—to fetch his purchases. "The supplies are too heavy for me to get out here in my condition, but you boys shouldn't have a problem."

Katie was amazed at the burlap sacks that came into camp then. She would have to find room in the two wagons after supper because there was certainly no room for that much now. Perhaps she could give some of the older flour and bacon to other families who couldn't afford to purchase much. It seemed like the right thing to do.

She walked over to Hannah, the preacher's wife, and asked her who in camp needed more food, and with Hannah's help, she determined who she would be gifting their older flour and bacon to. The former captain had purchased so much that they wouldn't have to worry about food for the rest of the journey—though they would be forced to eat some of the beans everyone dreaded.

Katie hated the beans as much as everyone else did, but she did her best to stay positive about the dreaded meal. It helped everyone to eat the beans, whether they wanted to or not.

Anna came over to the fire where Katie was cooking supper, peering into the large skillet she was cooking in. "Yes, Anna?"

"We're not having beans!"

Katie laughed. "We're going to have beans a lot before we reach Oregon City."

"But...didn't Mr. Bedwell get more food?"

"He did. The problem is he couldn't get a lot of meat, because it would go bad. Instead, he got things like flour and cornmeal. We can eat those things, but we need meat or beans to go with them."

Anna sighed dramatically. "I hope we're almost there then."

"Oh, sweetie. We've only been traveling for three months. We still have months to go."

Anna kicked a clump of dirt. "I like being with my friends on the trail, but I hate not having better food." It was as close to a tantrum as her daughter ever got, so instead of chastising her, Katie felt a bit pleased.

Katie smiled. "None of us like eating beans so much, Anna, but we are doing what we must. If I told you we had no food left but beans, you'd eat them with no problem."

"I suppose." Anna saw her friends and raised a hand in a wave. "I'm going to go play!"

Katie watched her daughter go, wishing she had the kind of energy the girl displayed. She'd walked all day, and now she'd play all night long.

George finished instructing the boys with the bags of food and sat down on a bench that had been built around a spot where there was a campfire. "This spot has been camped in more than most of the places we stay," he said, wondering if she'd keep her word and marry him the following evening. He didn't want to push her, but he wanted an answer. Hopefully, she wouldn't use his displays of temper in the past to keep from agreeing.

Just before calling the children to supper, Katie looked at George. "I think we should tell the children at supper that we'll be marrying tomorrow." Katie wished her heart was happier with the decision, but she knew it was best for her children. It would be too hard for a widow and four children to run a ranch together, no matter how much she'd tried to convince the children otherwise.

George smiled at her. "I'd like that a lot. We can tell them all at once. Are you still willing to marry tomorrow?"

Katie frowned. "Are you certain you don't mind not consummating the marriage? I worry that you think things will drastically change with our marriage, and I'm just not ready for that."

"But you think you will be eventually?" he asked. He knew Katie was marrying him for the help she needed to keep going and to start a ranch when they finally arrived at their destination. But he was marrying for love. He'd fallen in love for the first time in his life to the only woman who'd really stood up to him. Life was strange. Even a month ago, he would have said that a good wife was a compliant wife. Katie had taught him differently.

Katie nodded. "If not while we're on the trail, then once we settle. I can't tell you when I'll be ready, of course, but it's something that will eventually happen."

George wanted more, but he knew better than to ask for it. "That sounds just fine to me."

When the children gathered for supper, George immediately told them of their plans. "Mrs. Gabriel and I will be getting married tomorrow," he said.

Harvey looked surprised, but he was the only one. "Tomorrow evening?" he asked.

"Yes."

Anna asked the question that had been foremost on Katie's mind. "What will we call Mr. Bedwell then?"

George frowned, his eyes meeting Anna's. "Why don't you simply call me George like your mother does? And boys, you may begin to call Mrs. Gabriel Katie."

Katie amended his answer. "If you feel like calling George Father or Pa, you may. I don't want you to think that would be wrong. It's up to you. And Harvey and Albert, call me Katie or some form of Mother. I don't mind either way."

Harvey nodded. "That makes it easier."

Jane joined them then. "This looks like an important discussion," she said.

Katie smiled at her friend. "We've just told the children that we'll be marrying tomorrow," she said.

"Oh, that's wonderful!"

Katie went back to being all business then. "I made steaks from our venison, and I fried up some potatoes to go with it. I hope that sounds good to everyone." She was thrilled George had been able to purchase more potatoes. Most of the ones she had were sprouting, and though she'd keep them for seed, she would prefer fresh to cook with.

Jane's eyes widened. "Oh, yes. That sounds wonderful!"

Katie was pleased to see that Jane had her appetite back. She'd been worried about the other woman's lack of ability to eat while she was expecting.

She fixed plates for everyone, and they were passed around.

"I want to cook supper for you tomorrow, Katie," Jane said. "Anna can help me. That way you don't have to worry about cooking on your wedding day."

"Oh, I don't know about that," Katie said. "You're still expecting."

"I am, but I can help just this once."

Finally, Katie agreed. She could hear her mother whispering in her ear that it was all right to let someone bless you with kindness. If you always refused, you were taking their blessing from them. "All right. Thank you, Jane."

Jane was excited. "I don't know what I'll make, but perhaps we can do breakfast for supper. I'll make johnny cakes and bacon. Would that work?"

Katie knew her children would be excited about that, but she wasn't sure about George and his boys. "Sounds good to me," she said, her eyes meeting George's.

"As long as it's not...as long as it's food, my boys and I will eat it happily."

Katie knew what the man was going to say. He had almost said "as long as it's not beans." Katie was pleased that he rephrased though. It helped the whole family be willing to eat the meal when she had to make it.

After supper, Katie sat with George again, while the children wandered off after hearing Katie's admonitions to stay in camp that evening. She was a bit worried about the Indians, even though she'd heard they didn't usually attack the emigrants. It still felt better to have the children within the circle of the wagons. It quieted her fears of the heathens.

Chapter Eight

Tuesday, July 6th, 1852

Today is my wedding day. It's funny, but I don't feel at all like I did on my first wedding day, where I was nervous and blushing and excited to be able to share a bed and make a home with the man I loved.

This time, I'm thankful that there will be a way for my family to survive, but I still worry I'm making a mistake. Ned was a gentle man. He was kind and caring and loving to those around him. He changed diapers when he was home, and in the middle of the night when the babies cried, he brought them to me to nurse.

George is the exact opposite. He thinks he should be in charge of everyone around him. He has a temper that has curled the hair of half the women in our company. If a baby cried during the night, I doubt he would even wake, because he wouldn't care if a child cried. Well, he'd be annoyed it was interrupting his sleep if he did happen to wake.

How am I marrying a man who is the exact opposite of the man I loved and was so happy with? Is it even possible for me to be happy or content with George? I truly don't know.

With Ned, everything was good. Our lovemaking was...well...calm, if that makes any sense. When Ned touched me, I felt cared for and loved. When George touches me, it's different. It feels a little dangerous. I...I fear that I'm making a mistake marrying a man who is so different from me, but I don't think I can back out now. Not when we've told the children the wedding will happen today, and Jane has agreed to cook for my family...and...

I worry that I'm making a mistake, but if I am, I believe it's a good mistake to make. I love my children and having a man in their lives will be a good thing, if only George is able to keep his temper in check. I know he has much to teach my boys, and he will take the role as teacher seriously. I do hope he also keeps in mind that I never want him yelling at my children. I have to draw a line somewhere, and that must be my line.

My children have been given into my care by a loving God. They need to be treated with that kind of love from both of their parents, and George is stepping into the role of their father. Oh, I pray daily that this is not a mistake I'm making.

If all else fails, the children and I will disappear once we reach Oregon City, and no one will ever know I was married to George. I think that has to be my plan. There is an escape if things turn bad.

Before they left for their daily journey on Tuesday morning, everyone made sure their water barrels were full. It would be three days before they met up with the Bear River, the next body of water on their journey.

Katie fell into step with the other women as the wagons rolled out, and she was particularly quiet. She was either doing the best possible thing she could do or the absolute worst. It was strange to think of them both as being the same thing, but it was the case.

Word had gotten round that she was marrying, and Hannah moved beside her. "Are you nervous about your wedding this evening?"

Katie shrugged, but realized her friend deserved a real answer. "I am. I feel like this is the right thing to do for my children, unless he reverts to yelling at people all the time, in which case, I'll need to take my babies and run from him." She rubbed the back of her neck, wishing there was someone there to guide her and tell her exactly what to do.

Hannah nodded. "I understand exactly what you mean. I've talked to Jed about it, and he feels like he's seen a real change in Mr. Bedwell since he jumped into the river to save Anna. I believe you've seen the same."

Katie nodded. "I have. I just worry that it won't be enough of a change when it comes down to it. He'll be the one teaching my boys to ranch and helping them become men. I never would have chosen someone like George."

"Mr. Bedwell certainly knows a lot about survival and how to take care of the land and animals. He will be able to teach your boys a great deal."

"I know he will." Katie felt good that Hannah was even willing to admit there may have been a change. "Thank you."

"What can I do to help you? Could the children all sleep in our camp tonight?" Hannah asked.

"No, thank you," Katie said. She didn't feel like she had the right to share what her arrangement was with George, but there would be no intimacy that night. Not for a good long while as far as she was concerned.

"Well, I want to do something. I could cook supper for you. I'm not as good of a cook as I hear you are, but I'm more than happy to make a meal."

Katie shook her head. "Jane has already agreed to cook for us tonight. I really don't think there's anything I need other than peace of mind and that will have to come with time."

Hannah frowned at her. "Well, there must be something. Why don't I make you a dessert for tonight? Then you can have a nice meal *and* dessert. I'm sure your children would be thrilled."

Katie smiled at her friend, nodding. "That would be wonderful." *She couldn't take away her friend's blessing.*

Hannah looked excited. "I didn't think I'd be able to come up with anything you needed!"

"Well, you did, and my children and George's will both be happy." Katie sighed. "I hate that we won't have the safety of the river beside us for a while."

"I know," Hannah said. "We all rely on the water so much. Did you fill your barrels before leaving?" Everyone in camp had been told they needed to fill their water barrels, but there were times when people were forgotten.

"Yes, George made sure there were two full barrels for each wagon." And Harvey had made certain Jane's barrels were full.

"I guess you'll be one of the few couples who will need to keep two wagons. You'll be the mother of six when you marry."

Katie shook her head. "It sounds like so many. Ned and I always wanted at least five children, though, so it shouldn't seem that way. I think it's just jumping from four to six that feels so strange."

Penelope walked over to join them, Trudie at her side. "Is everyone going to the wedding tonight, or will it just be a few close friends?" Penelope asked. Katie could tell what Penelope was really asking was whether she could come to the wedding.

Katie bit her lip. "I suppose everyone can come. We all need reasons to celebrate, don't we?"

"Well, we did just celebrate Independence Day as well as your birthday," Trudie said, "but it will be nice to have something else soon. I feel like the worst part of the trail is the drudgery and boredom. We can't do things as we did back home."

Phillip came running to Katie then. "Mama, I found another book!"

Katie laughed. "Have you finished the last one?"

Phillip nodded. "I did. May I trade again?"

"As long as you only have one book in the wagon at any given time, and you're not walking and reading, I don't mind if you switch books. Next time you don't even have to ask."

Phillip threw his arms around her. "Thank you, Mama!" He ran ahead to the wagon to fetch his book, and then she saw him running back toward wherever he'd seen the new book.

Katie shrugged at her friends who looked at her oddly. "My Phillip would rather read than do anything else. Someone has been leaving books along the trail, and he takes whatever book he has in the wagon, and he switches with the book left there. That way he's not bringing a bunch of books, but he always has a new one to read." Katie knew she'd told Betty about the books, but she wasn't certain if she'd told the other women.

Penelope smiled. "I think that's a wonderful idea. People should be encouraging their children to participate in things like that. Perhaps other children in the company have the same dilemma, where they were only allowed to bring one book, and they've already read it too many times."

"I should suggest that to Phillip. He would probably love to trade books with his friends. It would be nice if he wasn't constantly looking for something else to read."

Trudie looked ahead of them. "I know you're worried about not traveling near water for a couple of days, but we're supposed to be crossing Big Hill this week. It's the most treacherous mountain crossing of our entire journey."

Katie sighed. "I thought crossing the North Platte River was supposed to be the most dangerous part of our journey."

"From what I read, it's the North Platte River, the Snake River, and Big Hill," Penelope said, staring ahead. "One out of three is over, but Big Hill is next. The valley on the other side is supposed to be a great place to camp for a day or two after the crossing, plenty of water, trees, fresh berries. Everything should be wonderful...except getting there."

Katie shook her head. "We'll make it. The men know what they're doing."

Trudie nodded. "The current captains have both read books about the trail. The former captain is the only one who has actually been this way before, and he may need to be consulted a great deal before we attempt it." She looked at Katie. "I think that means it's your job to soften him up and make him willing to give advice."

"How far from this Big Hill are we?" Katie asked.

"We should be there within the week. If you watch the men, they're all very serious and nervous about it. They're all acting differently." Penelope shrugged. "Herbert is ready to do what needs to be done. He said we'll have to tie the wheels and let the wagons slide down the slope, in some places, we'll have to have men with ropes slowly lowering the wagons."

"That sounds like it's very steep!" Katie said.

Trudie nodded. "It's a dangerous hike down the hill from what I understand. But getting the wagons down is the truly frightening part."

Katie vowed then not to let Anna out of her sight. The child was a bit of a daredevil, and she may just decide to roll down the hill. Phillip would want to read as he walked along, and he would fall down tumble bumble. Oh, the worries of going down a hill like that.

When they stopped for the noon meal, Katie asked George about Big Hill and the dangers that went with it. George removed his hat and scratched his head, seeming to think carefully about his response. "I won't lie and say it's not dangerous. It's a scary hill to go down. I've never walked down one steeper. No one will drive the wagons, and the oxen will have to be led down. The men will take care of getting the wagons and oxen down, but the women and children still need to make it down the hill. It won't be easy, but we can do it without losing any lives."

Katie shook her head. "That doesn't sound like it's anything I want my children involved with."

George took her hand in his. "I'll make sure our boys and wagons—including Jane's—get down that hill. You take care of the small children, and everything will be good."

Katie closed her eyes and took a deep breath. All she could see behind her lids was Anna rolling down a steep hill. "All right."

All day, all Katie could think about was getting over Big Hill. The very thought of it frightened her. She hoped no one would push for them to do twenty miles the day they went over the hill.

By the time they'd stopped for the day, she was in a tizzy, thinking about the dangers she faced with her children. Never had her urge to turn around and return to the east been stronger—not even when Ned had died.

George found her while the boys unhitched the oxen and took them to the area where they would be guarded for the night. He took one look at her face and understood what was happening.

"Katie, you can't fret over what's going to happen in a week. You have to face every day as it comes on the trail. There's no other way to do it without losing your mind."

"I feel like I lost mine the day I agreed to go to Oregon!" She shook her head. "How am I going to feel if I lose one of the children?"

"I'll talk to the captains and see if they're willing to have a meeting about Big Hill before we get there. Then we'll all know what to expect and how to handle things. Would that make you feel better?" he asked.

She nodded. "I think it would."

"Then I'll go and talk to them now. After I've finished, we'll wander over to the preacher and get married."

Katie smiled. She'd almost forgotten it was her wedding day in her worries over going over Big Hill. Why hadn't she been told about it? She was certain Ned would have known because he'd read so much about the trail. Had he hidden it from her so she wouldn't worry the whole way there?

When George came back to her a few minutes later, she'd started their campfire, and was poking at the flames with a long stick. The children were off gathering buffalo chips, and she would soon have more than she knew what to do with.

George squatted beside her at the fire. "I talked to Cauldron. He said he's planning to have a meeting the day before we reach Big Hill. We'll ford Thomas Fork of the Bear River, and then do the hill all in one day. It will only be about eight to ten miles of walking, but it will be one of the hardest days we've had. I told him how we'd made it over the hill when I was last on the trail, and he agreed to let me talk to the others and even direct the men on the crossing. Does that make you feel better?"

Katie nodded, but she wasn't so sure that it did help her to feel better. Her precious children would still be walking down a hill so steep that it would be frightening for them.

"Let's go get married then. Do you want the children there? Or just us?"

"I told some of the ladies that they were welcome to come to our wedding, so we have to have the children there. I'll gather them, and then we'll go."

As George watched, Katie got to her feet and raised her arm in the air. The children hurried from all parts of camp to gather around her, waiting for her instruction, even his own. George realized that his boys already obeyed Katie better than they ever had their own mother. It was as if she put some sort of spell over them, teaching them to be obedient.

"We're about to walk over to the preacher and get married. I thought you would all like to be there."

Anna held up both hands, which were filled with flowers. "I brought you flowers to carry, Mama, and I have flowers too, because I'm the only girl."

Katie hadn't really thought about her little Anna being the only girl with five brothers, but she smiled. Anna would have trouble courting anyone, because she would have five big brothers watching out for her. It sounded like the perfect situation to Katie.

As they all walked across the circle of the wagons to the pastor and his wife, Jed smiled, removing his hat. "Are you ready for the wedding then?" he asked.

Katie nodded. "Let's wait a few minutes though. There are women who said they wanted to attend, so we'll give them time to see you surrounded by people. I think they're all smart enough to realize what you're doing quickly."

Jed laughed. "I'm amazed at the intelligence of the women in this company. Of course, my wife loves all of you."

Katie glanced around, and then she saw Hannah standing off to one side, giving her a smile of encouragement. Katie gave a timid smile back, wishing the whole thing was just over with for the day. She didn't want to have to even think about her wedding night.

Within five minutes, most of the company was there to observe their vows. George was a bit baffled that people would come to his wedding to support him after the way he'd acted, but Katie seemed to take it all in stride. Of course, she did. She was the real reason people were there. They cared about her, not about him.

Before they knew what was happening, the wedding was over, and Jed said, "You may kiss the bride."

Katie obediently raised her lips to George, expecting a quick peck on the lips, but George gave her a real kiss, the type she'd only ever shared with Ned. And to Katie's surprise, she liked it more than she'd ever liked a kiss with Ned. A tingling feeling spread throughout her body, and she leaned toward George, inviting him to deepen the kiss.

At the sound of Jed clearing his throat, she jumped away from George, her eyes on the ground. She hadn't expected to like his kiss so much, and she was extremely embarrassed that it had been obvious to everyone watching how very much she'd enjoyed it.

She politely thanked Jed for his time, and took Anna's hand, leading the girl back to camp.

George stared after his wife and new daughter, wondering if he'd done something wrong. Kissing had never felt so right.

Chapter Nine

Wednesday, July 7th, 1852

I'm married again, but this time, I'm married to a woman I love. She is very afraid of crossing Big Hill, and it has given me the opportunity to go to the new captains of our company and try to make amends. The other men have read about this crossing, but I'm the only one in the group who has personally experienced it. The new captains have given me permission to lead the men on the crossing of the hill, which will allow me to apologize to our company in a huge way.

I was surprised at the sheer number of people who attended my wedding to Katie, but it didn't take long to realize they were all there for her. She is friends with almost every woman in the group. I have made one friend since leaving Independence, and I married her.

I didn't realize it at the time but jumping into the river to save little Anna Gabriel has changed my life in more ways than I could have imagined. It was a split-second decision, and I'm glad I did it, because it brought Katie and her children into my life. I already love her children, but not nearly as much as I love my Katie.

She doesn't yet consider herself my Katie, but that's all right. She will before too terribly long. I hope that seeing me lead the men for a day will help her see that I'm a changed man, and I am truly trying to help others in every way that I can.

Her sons are very responsible for their ages—more responsible than my boys, I'm sorry to say. The love she's shown them is much more powerful than the fear I instilled in my boys. Even they have remarked about how much I've changed, and I will follow her example in parenting for the rest of my days.

I never thought I would want to be the parent of a girl, but I love little Anna. She is dear to me in a way I didn't think a girl could be. I don't know if the connection is from my saving her or from something else, but I just want to wrap her in cotton and buy her porcelain dolls.

I asked if they had any dolls at Fort Bridger, but they didn't. I guess I'll have to wait until we get to Oregon City, which is still months away. I do wish we could all arrive faster. A child Anna's age shouldn't have to walk across the entire continent. I'll make sure she never goes on a journey such as this again.

It was strange to go to sleep beside George on their wedding night, but he made no move to touch her as promised. Instead, they lay beside one another in the tent she shared with Anna, while all the boys were in the other tent.

Ned, I've married again, but I promise I haven't given my heart to George. I have married him for the sake of our children. They need a father, though I couldn't have found one more different than you. I hope you will forgive me for what I feel is a betrayal, but I'm doing what I must. I will always love you, Ned, but I won't be talking to you every night anymore. My loyalty must be with my new husband. I have to build a new life with him, no matter how it hurts to feel as if I'm leaving you behind.

On Wednesday morning, Katie made flapjacks and bacon for breakfast, and they talked about Big Hill a little bit more. The boys hadn't yet heard about it, but George explained what it would be like to have to drive the oxen up the hill, but worse, how to get the wagons down the hill.

Stanley's eyes were wide as they talked about it, but Phillip just grinned. "Perhaps I should put my book down before we start walking that day."

Katie frowned at her son. "Don't even joke about that! I close my eyes and I see you and your sister tumbling down the hill."

Gregory immediately said, "I'll watch out for Phillip if you can watch out for Anna."

Katie smiled, thankful her son would offer such a thing. "I would greatly appreciate that, Gregory. Both of them need to be watched going down that hill." Her two younger children were rather clumsy, and she worried so much about them.

Stanley nodded. "I'll do as George tells me and make sure our wagon and all of our belongings make it to the bottom. I know we can do it."

George nodded at Stanley. "Good man."

At the use of the word man, Katie was certain Stanley's chest grew by five inches. She would have to thank George later for being so good with her eldest son.

Albert nodded. "I'll work with Stanley. Together we're strong enough to do a man's job."

"That would be good," Stanley said.

"We'll all look after each other and make it safely over the hill and down the other side," George said, proud of how this new family was merging together and offering to help one another.

Katie watched it all happen around her, and she knew that she was raising fine children—and George's were learning how to care for others and not just look out for themselves as well. She was very proud.

When they began their walk that day, Katie found herself between Trudie and Penelope again, and she told them what she'd found out about Big Hill and how they were already readying their children for it mentally.

Penelope smiled. "Believe it or not, I feel safer knowing that Mr. Bedwell will be in charge of our Big Hill crossing. I trust the current captains, but neither of them has gone over that particular hill, and it sounds like something we need to have knowledgeable men who respect the hill in charge of."

Trudie nodded. "I wouldn't want Mr. Bedwell in charge of the entire journey, because we all know how that worked out, but I do like the idea of him taking charge of Big Hill. It sounds like it's the smartest thing to do."

Katie felt as if a huge weight was off her shoulders as they talked about the hill every day, all of them knowing that it was coming, and they would be working together to stay safe.

By Thursday afternoon, they had connected with the Bear River and replenished their water supply. It always felt safer to Katie to have water readily available, even if they couldn't drink it just as water.

They would travel along the river until they had to ford it on Saturday morning. At least that's what they were projecting, but there was no telling when there would be another huge storm coming in.

Another couple was lost to cholera on Friday, and they had three children. Katie longed to take in the extra children, but she already had six. She asked George about it, and he said she could do it if she wanted, but they ended up going to the pastor and Hannah. They were good people and would be wonderful parents to the young orphans.

Before bed on Friday night, Katie asked George if they could pray for a safe crossing as a family. Both for the river the next morning but also for Big Hill. After being nervous about it for most of the week, she was pleased it was all going to be over with soon, and then she would just worry about the Snake River later in their journey.

George said a prayer for all of them, and after the children were asleep, he whispered to her, "Make sure you keep hold of Anna's hand the entire time we're crossing the river in the morning. There's no reason for her to be off on her own, and I can't be sure someone will be close enough to jump in after her this time."

Katie agreed wholeheartedly. "She doesn't get too close to the rivers unless we're crossing one, and then her curiosity gets the better of her."

He sighed. "Let's just make sure to keep her safe. I'll have Albert looking out for her as well, and he's a strong swimmer."

"Thank you for that. I appreciate all you do to keep our children safe."

George smiled when she said, "our children" instead of "my children." It felt right to him. "I will always do my duty as their father." He reached for her, touching her the first time since the wedding, and cupped her face in his hands. Kissing her softly, he felt closer to her than ever before. Hopefully soon, she would be ready to be intimate with him. He was waiting for the day.

Katie woke earlier than usual the following morning and decided to make a good breakfast for her family. Usually she didn't do anything special, but she wanted everyone to have a good start to their day.

First, they had to ford the stream, an offshoot of the Bear River, and then they'd be heading up and over Big Hill. Katie could see it past the river but off in the distance.

Having camped at the side of the stream, it looked particularly muddy and steep. Crossing it would be difficult, and that was before they even got to Big Hill. The whole day would be nerve wracking, and it would be all she could do to let go of her worries, and put them in God's hands, but she would pray the whole way, and it would work out. It had to.

George ended up being the one to explain about the difficult stream crossing to the captains, who instructed the others. They'd also let everyone know that it would be George giving the orders when it came to Big Hill.

The day was long, and the journey was arduous. After fording the stream—and poor Jane losing her bag of flour—they spent the rest of the morning moving along to the foot of Big Hill, where they stopped for their noon meal. The noon meal that day was unlike any other they'd had along the route. George got up and explained the way they would have to tie the wheels and lower the wagons with ropes at one point to get down Big Hill.

To Katie's surprise, everyone listened to him carefully, and seemed ready to follow George as a leader once again. Perhaps he had actually changed enough that others in the group were noticing it.

After their noon meal, they began the steep walk up the hill. Katie was out of breath by the time she was halfway to the top, and she noticed most of the other women were as well. Anna stayed at her side, though she didn't understand the necessity, and all of the children wanted to be together. That day, none of the mothers would allow their children to go off alone as they usually did. It was much too difficult.

The way down the other side was even more frightening for Katie, having to watch where she put each of her feet as she carefully walked down the hill. Her foot slipped more than once, and she wanted to simply sit down on the side of the hill and cry, giving up the pretense of being strong enough to make it to the bottom.

Each time she thought about giving up, she looked at Anna's face, and she knew she had to make it to the bottom of the hill in one piece for her children.

She couldn't pay any attention at all to the wagons as they were coming down, because the way was so steep. There was little chatting as they all watched their footing descending the hill.

When Katie had finally reached the bottom, she stood and watched the wagons being lowered, so many of the men working to lower them over a certain point. She was grateful that part wasn't hers, and every time she looked, George was with another wagon, helping belongings be secured or guiding the oxen over a difficult point.

She knew they planned to camp at the bottom of the hill, so she had Anna, Gregory, and Phillip begin to gather buffalo chips. Gregory had been given the important task of carrying the family rifle to the bottom of the hill, and once they were there, Katie told him he may go ahead and load it and look for game. It would keep him busy and out of the way.

Most of the women sat down and watched their husbands and wagons come down the hill slowly and carefully. Not one wagon slipped as Katie watched, and she couldn't help but be proud of George. All of the wagons had made it safely to the bottom of Big Hill, and he hadn't once lost his temper. He seemed pleased with everyone, and as he watched, he walked from man to man, telling them all what a great job they'd done getting the wagons and the oxen down the hill.

There had only been one injury in the entire company, and that was Mr. Henderson. He'd slipped and sprained his ankle, but others jumped in to help him, and he'd made it down safely anyway. He'd have a hard time for a few days, but since his wife had died, everything had been hard for him anyway.

Jed stood up and walked to the middle of the people who had gathered and said, "Let's thank our Lord for getting us through one of the most difficult parts of our journey in one piece."

Katie felt tears streaming down her cheeks as she listened to the pastor's words of thanksgiving. All her worry had been for nothing. Her family was safe and sound, and they were at the bottom of the hill she'd been fretting about for days.

After the prayer, Katie heard a gunshot, and she looked. There was Gregory standing over a deer he'd shot. Stanley, Albert, and Harvey looked like they'd been beaten, but they all went to help Gregory get the animal back to camp.

George stood up and smiled. "I'm proud of the work we did together today, and I would like to share the venison my son just shot with the entire company. We can all have fresh meat tonight. I think perhaps the women could make us a few huge pots of stew to share."

Katie's heart leapt when George called her Gregory his son. It felt right to be married to him now, and she knew it was time to tell him she was willing to be intimate with him. It had been hard lying beside him every night and not touching him. The man...well, he made her heart pound in ways that surprised her.

Katie, Margaret, and Trudie all took out their largest pots and each started a fire. They would be the ones to cook the stew that night. Each of them used huge portions of the venison, and people brought what they had to spare—potatoes, carrots, and flour. Several of the other women made biscuits to go with the stew, and within a couple of hours of finishing their descension, they had a hearty meal, and everyone shared.

It was Saturday, so the band played for them, and they danced. It felt like more of a celebration than the Fourth of July had to Katie, because they were celebrating still being alive after their difficult day.

While the dancing took place, Katie took George's hand and took him for a walk, after letting Harvey, Albert, and Stanley know they would be gone for a while.

George was surprised at Katie's desire to be alone with him, but he certainly didn't complain that she wanted to spend time with him without the children. That didn't happen nearly often enough.

After they were well out of hearing of the camp, she said, "I'm so proud of how you did today. Your leadership is what the entire company needed."

He smiled. "I almost lost my temper once, but I used your fruits of the spirit, and it worked perfectly."

"Why did you almost lose your temper?" Katie hadn't noticed anything untoward happening, and no one had said anything to her, so he must have done well with controlling himself.

He shrugged. "One of the men thought he should be able to drive his oxen down the hill the way he'd driven everywhere else. He finally agreed to do things my way, but it took some convincing."

Katie shook her head. "You would think he'd want to do what would more likely leave him alive at the bottom of the hill."

"So many families have lost loved ones on this journey that I think we should all work together as much as we can."

She squeezed his hand. "I agree. And I realized something when we all made it to the bottom of the hill…"

"What's that?"

She took a deep breath, hating that she'd have to blurt out what she was thinking, but what other way was there to tell him? "I think I'm ready to be intimate with you." Wanting to look down at the ground so he couldn't see her face, Katie forced herself to keep her head up, even though she was embarrassed.

He stared at her for a moment, shocked by her words. Patience had never been willing to suffer his romantic attentions, and here Katie was, telling him she was willing. "Are you certain?" he asked. "I mean, I want to throw you down right here in the grass and have my way with you, but I also don't want to do anything you're not comfortable with."

Katie wrapped both of her arms around him. "I'm certain. I realized today my world would be so much worse without you in it. I'm glad you made it safely to the bottom of that hill."

He leaned down and kissed her softly. "So am I."

Chapter Ten

Sunday, July 11th, 1852

We made it through two of the most difficult passages of our journey yesterday, though there will be more soon. I feel safe with my family.

George led the company over Big Hill, and he did a wonderful job, reclaiming some of the respect he had at the beginning of the journey. I'm proud to call him my husband, and quite pleased with how well he guided everyone.

My boys are happy with my marriage and are already looking to George as a father-figure, and my Anna has already looked up to him because he saved her when she fell into the North Platte River. I have made a wise decision with my marriage, and today I look forward to a day of rest. I cannot wait for the journey to be over, but I've begun another journey this week, and I must admit I've done the right thing.

George kissed Katie with passion, slowly lowering her to the ground where they had walked. It was dark, and they wouldn't be seen from camp, so he let himself go, making sweet love to the lady he had chosen to be his forever love.

As he kissed her, he was surprised by her responses to him. Patience had always lain still and closed her eyes, telling him to get on with it. She had been the only woman in his life before Katie, and now he realized how much he'd been missing in his bedroom with his wife.

Katie though, she had obviously made love with someone she loved, and she knew where she liked to be touched, guiding his lips to her breasts, and his hand to the spot between her legs. She gasped and responded to his every touch in a way that made him feel that she wasn't just doing this for him—she was also doing it for herself.

When he joined them together, he kissed her once more, telling her that she was his entire world. As he climaxed, he whispered over and over, "I love you, Katie. I love you."

Katie lay on the ground beside her husband, shocked that he'd told her he loved her. When he'd asked her to marry him, he'd made it seem that he wanted marriage for the same reasons she had. For a mother for his boys, and to make life easier on the trail.

But he loved her. It would take some time for that to sink in for her, and she would need to think about exactly how she felt about him as well.

As they walked back to camp to join their children, she snuggled into his side, thrilled to be with him. He made her feel things physically that she'd never felt with Ned, and it seemed odd those feelings would come alive with George, whom she wasn't even certain how she felt about.

When they got to camp, Harvey was waiting up for them. "We took a vote, and we're traveling tomorrow. There's a great spot for us to camp in just about eleven more miles. We'll move in the morning, have our church service after the noon meal, and then we will stay over there for two or three days to rest before moving on."

George nodded. "I know the spot, and it's a good one." It wasn't how he'd handle things because he wanted to be in Oregon City as early in the year as possible, but he couldn't fault the other captains. Clover Creek was definitely a beautiful place to rest for a few days.

They climbed into their tent with Anna, and for the first time, George slept with his new wife in his arms. He hadn't been able to miss the fact that she hadn't told him she loved him back, but perhaps love would grow within her for him. He hoped so anyway.

As they walked the next morning, they passed a small trading post run by a man who called himself Peg-Leg Smith. He asked if anyone had anything to sell to him and showed them what he had. His wife was an Indian woman, and Katie looked at the woman curiously. She'd never been this close to an Indian, but the woman didn't seem to want to kill them, so all was good. It seemed odd to her that a white man would marry an Indian woman, but the two seemed happy together.

Thankfully, they were able to replace the flour Jane had lost in the river crossing before they moved on toward Clover Creek.

They reached Clover Creek by noon the following day, and they set up camp using the firepits that had been there from previous emigrants. The creek was good for their laundry, and the entire area was filled with wild berries. Katie definitely understood why the captains wanted to stay there longer.

After their church service, Katie and Jane walked away from camp together, carrying their baskets with them. They were able to find chokecherries, currants, and elderberry along the creek.

When they returned to camp, Katie immediately started to roll out the crusts for three pies, and the women worked together to turn the chokecherries and elderberry into pies. "Would you mind if I took a pie over to the Hendersons?" Jane asked. "The children lost their mother, and now their father is injured. I just feel like they need to have someone watch out for them."

"Of course not!" Katie said. "I think that's a good idea."

George and the boys went hunting with the other men in camp and they returned with three deer. Katie had a hard time believing just what a wonderful area she'd come to. She knew she wanted to make her home there, though there were no settlers nearby.

After starting supper, she wandered around to the other fires and spoke to the other women, who all agreed. Clover Creek was where they wanted to make their home. It was close to the Mormon territory but not actually part of it, so it seemed safe enough. None of the women wanted their men getting any ideas from the Mormons that they should have more than one wife.

As they sat down for supper that evening, George thanked God for giving them such a beautiful place to camp that was plentiful with fruit and deer for their cookpots.

The children were quite excited by the pies, and Anna said they should live in the beautiful valley where they'd landed.

"It's called Bear Lake Valley," George told them all. "It's everyone's favorite place to camp in the area. Beautiful, isn't it?"

Anna nodded. "Can we live here? Please, Pa?"

Katie froze for a moment. It was the first time one of her children had called George Pa, but it made sense that it would be Anna whose life George had saved.

"I think that's a great idea, but I know your Ma is planning to live near the other families in our company, so you'll have friends as soon as we settle."

Katie smiled at that. "I've already talked to the other women. We all want to settle here. With a lake nearby, the creek for water and fishing, I cannot think of a place that would be better."

George laughed. "This is where I was planning on settling with my family, even before I met you." He was surprised she and the other women agreed to live right where he wanted to live.

"Well, that's settled then, isn't it?"

"And we will be soon...right here!" Harvey said with a sly grin.

"I suppose we will. This is the perfect place for all of us, I think," Katie said. "I'll make as many pies as we can pick berries for."

"They have huckleberries around here too, but we have to go up into the mountains to find those."

"I've never even tried a huckleberry," Katie said. "I like the idea of having a new fruit for all of us to enjoy." She sighed contentedly. There were still over nine hundred miles to go to reach Oregon City, and they all wanted to get back there before winter set in. It wasn't over by any means, but decisions had been made, and Clover Creek would someday be their home. It seemed like a silly thing to do, going that far and having to come back, but they couldn't homestead the land until they had staked their claim, and that had to be done in Oregon City.

After their supper, Katie and George walked. All day through their travels, through her berry picking, through all the daily chores a woman on the trail must perform, she'd been thinking. George Bedwell, the man she'd married, would be her forever. There was no running from him once they hit Oregon City and getting a frontier divorce. She loved him.

She didn't love the gruff man who'd yelled at her while she'd tried to care for him and help him recover from pneumonia. She loved the man who'd jumped into a raging river to save her daughter from drowning. The man who had taken over teaching her sons to hunt and to be men. She loved the George who had led their company over Big Hill.

After they were out of earshot of the camp, she went into his arms, very ready for his lovemaking. With George there was so much passion, she couldn't seem to stay away from him, while with Ned things had been comfortable.

They kissed and slowly sank to the ground, covered in green grass as opposed to the barren wasteland they'd just come through. After they made love, they lay in one another's arms there on the ground, not worrying about anything but being together.

George held her, stroking her bare arm, and telling her he loved her once again. Now that the words were out, there was no reason to hide how he felt. Everything about her was perfect to him. "I love you, Katie," he said. "I didn't know it was possible to love someone so much it hurt inside, but now I do. Thank you for agreeing to be my wife."

Katie propped herself up on her elbow, looking down at her husband by the light of the half moon. "I love you too, George. I have no idea how it happened, but you have become the husband and father my children and I needed."

He stared at her for a moment, not able to believe what she'd said. No one could love him. It wasn't possible. "You don't have to lie to me, Katie. I'm simply happy to know that you'll allow me to love you."

She shook her head, a smile touching her lips. "I do love you, though. I didn't expect to, but I do. I think watching how gently and ably you brought us all over Big Hill told me what I needed to know to love you. I watched you all day, and I couldn't help but think, 'That's my husband. He's wonderful.' And you *are* wonderful."

He pulled her down for another passionate kiss. "I'm so happy you gave me a chance. You make me want to be a better person, just by spending time with you. I thank you for that."

She shook her head. "You had a better person inside you, and you learned to stop being afraid to let him show. I can't wait to settle here and raise our family. Perhaps we can have another child, one who belongs to both of us."

He smiled. "I would like that more than I could ever tell you." He looked around him at the beautiful valley, and he thought he would try to get the very land they camped on for their ranch. It would be perfect.